Michael Hampson was ordained in the Church of England at the age of twenty-four, after reading Philosophy and Psychology at Oxford and training for ordination at Ripon College Cuddesdon. He served two years in Burnley in his native Lancashire and eleven years at Church Langley in Harlow, Essex. He now works full-time as a writer and retreat leader. www.michaelhampson.co.uk

Last Rites

The End of the
Church of England

MICHAEL HAMPSON

Granta Books
London

Granta Publications, 2/3 Hanover Yard, Noel Road,
London N1 8BE

First published in Great Britain by Granta Books 2006

A CIP catalogue record for this book is available
from the British Library.

1 3 5 7 9 10 8 6 4 2

ISBN-13: 978-1-86207-891-8
ISBN-10: 1-86207-8911-2

Typeset by M Rules
Printed and bound in Italy by Legoprint

CONTENTS

INTRODUCTION

Many great British institutions have faced crisis, but only the Church of England has created a situation where virtually all its energy is invested in self-defeating pursuits at every level of the organisation. At the national level the courteous rivalry between high church and low church has evolved into a public battle of mutual loathing between liberal and fundamentalist. At the local level most of what the clergy do with their time is actively counter-productive. Through the entire structure of the organisation, where there should be mutual respect and support, there is instead mutual suspicion and hostility. The finances are in chaos. The liturgy – the public worship of the church – is everywhere in disarray. Sunday attendance continues to fall at the rate of 25 per cent a decade, halving with each generation. The Church of England is no longer even the largest church in the land: in terms of Sunday attendance the Roman Catholic church in England is larger, and more united as well. From the national and regional institutions to the local parish church, the Church of England is an organisation in terminal crisis. Like a dying tree in its final months, it still has buds and leaves in places, but the trunk is rotten and much of the greenery turns out to be moss and poison ivy. The storm will come and the tree will fall.

I first enquired about ordination in 1981, at the age of fourteen. I was ordained ten years later, after three post-graduate years at one of the Church of England's most respected theological colleges. Those ten years were over-seen by inspiring people full of great vision for all that the church could be. We knew there were problems, but renewal was in the air. Morale was high throughout the institution. It seemed that everything was in place for the Church of England to become the soul of the nation for the next generation, as it had been for generations before. In reality the dead weight of its history would continue to drag the institution down ever further into its hopeless spiral of decline. I walked away thirteen years later. Half my college contemporaries had already left.

Throughout those thirteen years, disillusion and inspiration ran in parallel. I served my first two years as a curate in Burnley in Lancashire. I was taking fifty funerals a year, all of them for people I had never met. The most natural thing should have been to invite those families to join us week by week in church, but the Sunday services were so dull and uninspiring. I was the official representative and I didn't believe in the product. My inspiration there was a congregation that met in a school hall on a slowly developing new estate. Established by the previous vicar, it had moved on from being a meeting for school mums to being a small church in its own right. The present vicar wanted little to do with it, so it became the curate's domain. Across those two years the numbers attending doubled: the welcome team would be putting out extra chairs as the service began. We produced an attractive information card, reintroduced coffee after the service and held congregation meetings so that everybody felt involved.

After two years in Burnley the national Church Appointments Office matched me up with a vacancy in Harlow in Essex. A new phase of Harlow New Town, self-contained on a greenfield site, was to treble the population of Saint Mary Magdalene parish from five thousand to fifteen thousand. The new curate was to establish a new congregation in a multi-purpose building on the new estate, named Church Langley by the house builders' marketing team. Church Langley Church would be my focus for the next eleven years, seven as curate of the old parish of Saint Mary Magdalene, four as first vicar of the newly created parish of Church Langley. Those eleven years were the glory years, discovering all that the church could become in an entirely contemporary community. They were also the years during which the demands and expectations of the archaic culture and structures of the Church of England would weigh ever more heavily.

After eleven years at Church Langley it was the right time for a move. I was ready for a different challenge, but any post in any parish would mean continuing to live with the counter-productive demands and expectations of the national church, and the additional burden of an ancient building with pillars and pews. There was nowhere else to go in the Church of England to help develop a church appropriate for the present generation – those of us born in the last forty years – because the dead weight of the archaic institution is everywhere dragging it down.

In my own mind and in my own diary I fixed my leaving

date thirteen months in advance, allowing those months to change my mind, but from the day I made the decision I felt the burden lift and there was no going back.

With a year still to serve, I looked on like an outsider as the church launched itself into its most vitriolic and spiteful conflict to date. Nine English bishops wrote to the newspapers condemning the appointment of a gay man as the next Bishop of Reading, an unprecedented public undermining of their own archbishop. Their campaign continued even after they had extracted a promise of celibacy from the candidate. The appointment had been supported by the Archbishop of Canterbury and confirmed by Buckingham Palace. Now the archbishop forced Jeffrey John to write to the palace and resign. These events finally tore up the silent consensus under which thousands of gay clergy had operated in the church for centuries – myself included. If I had not already decided to leave I would have been wondering how long I could survive in this new era of open persecution. I realise now that the events marked not the end of one ministry or even many ministries, but another major step towards the final demise of the Church of England itself.

It is strange to recall that this collapsing institution was once one of the great civilising institutions of the nation, or that as recently as the 1980s it had unity and influence and purpose. Fighting for control of what remains are the liberals and the fundamentalists. Neither party represents or nourishes the laity in the parishes, and neither has any appeal to the nation at large. The fundamentalists vainly believe the church will survive their battle to take control. The liberals vainly trust that a thousand years of history guarantee a stable future and that the pendulum will swing in their direction once again.

This final battle is tragically unequal. The special talent of the liberals is to bring people together to work out a compromise and common ground; the special talent of fundamentalism is to get its own way. The liberals repeatedly compromise, and fundamentalism simply holds the line, until the liberals themselves are promoting the fundamentalist cause 'for the sake of unity'.

Last Rites takes a tour of this crumbling institution. It examines the liberals and the fundamentalists – who they are, where they come from and what they believe. It examines the people and the parishes and the structures – the dwindling congregations, the dispirited clergy, the chaotic finances, the burden of unsuitable buildings. It identifies the underlying causes of the current distress – the culture and structures of 'establishment' – and proposes a fundamental transformation in both culture and structure as the one hope for renewal. For the sake of the future church it is time to disestablish and dismantle what remains of the ancient Church of England.

PART I

The State We're In

CHAPTER 1

Vicarage Life

I first attended an ordination service just three years before my own ordination. As those who were being ordained processed to the centre of the cathedral it occurred to me that the human race has been doing this since the beginning of time: taking young people and declaring them to be ministers or priests for the service of the faith. We were taking part in a ceremony as universal as the air we breathe and as ancient as the hills, timeless and shared with the whole of humankind. Then my focus switched in a moment from the vast and the eternal to the immediate and the intimate. These young adults had been completing their training at theological college only the week before, and would be starting work in their parishes the next day. The bishop was declaring their responsibilities from that day forward: 'You must set the Good Shepherd always before you as the pattern of your calling. The treasure now to be entrusted to you is Christ's own flock.'

Three years later I was amongst those being ordained, and these were our hopes and our dreams. We would go out into the parishes to serve the faith at the heart of the community in the name of Jesus himself. It is the ancient and enduring self-image of the Church of England: to serve as the established church, the official religion of the land, the church of the whole nation, the church of every citizen, the church at least of those who do not actively opt out; to serve as part of the great and benevolent machinery of the English state. The Church of England dream is to be the soul of the nation.

We came from the kind of thriving parishes and undergraduate chaplaincies where everything seemed possible: where the main Sunday service was an event not to be missed, supplemented by mid-week prayer groups, Bible studies and informal communions; where everybody who attended was involved in creating a profound sense of community and belonging; where everything was top quality, from the music to the weekly bulletin, from the liturgy to the publicity, from the welcome to the preaching, from the plumbing to the decorating and the sound system and the heating, from the present moment to the future planning. Places like these are in a tiny minority: we were caught up in a dream that bore no relation to contemporary reality. We knew the national structures that made the newspapers, the kind of people who like to work with ordination candidates, and a small number of parishes where we had been members or had been on placement during training. We each knew the hopes and expectations of one highly partisan theological college, but there were fifteen other highly partisan colleges out there, each with its own set of hopes and expectations.

Out there in the mainstream parishes Sunday attendance had been in freefall for decades. We were about to be sent as curates to serve under vicars in relatively large parishes – parishes that could still justify having curates – but nationally there are just nine thousand salaried clergy for sixteen thousand church buildings. In most of those buildings fewer than forty adults gather each Sunday – most of them retired – and numbers continue to fall year by year. Just one church in six bucks the trend with an average Sunday attendance of more than a hundred. Two-thirds have fewer than fifty, one-third have fewer than twenty. These dwindling congregations are called upon not only to maintain those ancient buildings – at their own expense – but to meet almost the entire clergy salary bill as well.

The junk mail received by the clergy reveals the nature of those buildings. They need steeplejacks, stonemasons and organ builders. They need reroofing, repointing, repainting and rewiring. Even where all this is done they are hardly suitable for contemporary use. The pipe organ would not be the musical instrument of choice. The pew would not be the seating of choice. They still need new heating, new lighting, new plumbing. The congregation is left meeting in a museum with pillars and pews and the clutter of many decades. Changes to the building – even when they can be afforded – are controlled by an internal church system far stricter than planning regulations or listed-building controls. Fund-raising events come to dominate the parish diary. Last week's collection is reported on the weekly bulletin. Graphs of parish income and expenditure are fixed to prominent pillars. Envelope schemes, standing orders and Gift Aid are promoted. Clergy and lay people alike feel the responsibility and the strain.

At the heart of it all the main weekly event in that

building – the Sunday-morning liturgy – ought to be the sustaining glory of the church. In most places instead it combines the tedious with the embarrassing. The preaching is patronising in both presentation and content, the music is turgid and set too high, there are hierarchical processions of choir and clergy formalised to the point of sombre at the beginning and end, long passages of unfamiliar and unworthy text are read out loud from locally photocopied booklets and sheets, and attention is focused continuously on the miserable sinfulness of all those gathered from the opening prayers onwards. If you happen to attend a cheerful and upbeat church you find that frivolity and third-rate entertainment have replaced the liturgy: at Family Service, material designed poorly for seven-year-olds is ignored by children and parents of all ages as the latter try to control the former, and any non-parent over the age of eleven winces with embarrassment, either grinning through it or staring at the floor. In either format the whole sequence resembles a lecture for children of primary-school age, interrupted at random by the demand that everyone bow their head, or stand up to sing, or read out loud from a book. Both formats are suffering the same relentless decline in attendance year by year.

Bishop David Stancliffe is chairman of the Church of England Liturgical Commission. In his 2003 book *God's Pattern* he writes: 'how do worshippers manage to keep on going to church faithfully when the way worship is prepared and offered is often so dire; when it is frequently confused with entertainment; and when it is led by those who apparently have no idea about what they are doing or professional competence in doing it?'

About three years ago I took a long walk with an archdeacon friend, talking about my future plans and the state of the church. An archdeacon looks after a range of practical matters across fifty or a hundred parishes, especially during the vacancy between the last vicar and the next one. He confided that the greatest problem with filling vacancies was the quality of the applicants. He would rather keep posts vacant than fill them with those who applied. 'The problem is the quality of the clergy.'

On ordination day we were so full of ideals. We longed to share with others the love, joy and peace that we had found in our faith. We had built our lives on that faith and now we were committing our lives to serving the community of people who shared that faith. We saw ourselves building up those who gathered, reaching out to those who stayed away, and in all things celebrating the goodness of a God beyond compare. Most ended up dispirited, jaded, wearied and worn down, presiding over those dire Sunday mornings and talking in infant-school theology: more Noah's Ark than Jesus of Nazareth.

When I left after thirteen years, I was behind the game. Only a quarter of my college leavers' year completed those thirteen years in parish ministry. Another quarter left and then went back, with varying degrees of reluctance and various plans for the future. The rest have left with no intention of going back. They have worked for charities as front line service providers, and for the prison service and the health service as chaplains and managers. They have bluffed on their CVs to cover up their history. They have been unemployed and early-retired. They go to church rarely or not at all. Each year my old college sends its annual newsletter, now complete with a smiling group photograph of those about to be ordained, and I feel sorry for them for all that lies ahead.

The Church of England imposes a whole range of pressures on its clergy that convert them from their initial idealism to jaded exhaustion. It makes them live in vicarages – over-sized and badly maintained public buildings next to the churches they serve. It condemns them to work alone through anti-social hours up to fifteen hours a day. It burdens them with impossible expectations – to be everywhere at once, perfect in everything, infinitely creative. It imposes incompetent attempts at management, assessment and discipline, and burdens them with guilt over the decline of the church nationally and locally. But most of all it makes them live with the central Church of England fantasy: that the Church of England is still the soul of the nation, the church of every citizen, a welcome and appreciated presence in every English home, when it is not.

We live in a secularised and multicultural democracy. People know other religions better than they know Christianity. Other religions are more openly observed by their friends and colleagues, and are better taught in our schools. Christianity today occupies the same space on the fringes of mainstream culture as any other major or minor religious cult or claim from any continent – spiritualism, astrology, reincarnation – perhaps more respectable than Wicca or clairvoyance but less respectable than reiki or domestic feng shui. Included in this marketplace of contemporary beliefs and practices is the fading collective memory of a socially respectable English religion based in a long stone building with pillars, pews, a graveyard and a steeple. This is all that remains of 'the faith of the nation', but it still leads many engaged couples to seek a church wedding, a significant minority of new parents to request a christening, and almost all the bereaved to ask for a Church of England funeral. The clergy are left juggling two entirely incompatible roles: they work to develop the life of a congregation as a distinctive Christian community within a secular and multicultural society, and they are required by law to use Christian ceremonies to baptise, marry and bury people they have never met before and will never meet again, people who neither have nor wish to have any connection with that distinctive Christian community. The law favours the latter role above the former: baptising, marrying and burying are legal obligations; building up the congregation is not. The clergy are required by law to lead the main services every Sunday, but it makes no legal difference whether anybody attends. In one current example of extreme pastoral breakdown, the entire congregation has abandoned the vicar, to organise its own services in the village hall. The vicar carries on in church regardless, fulfilling his legal duty and drawing his salary. The bishop has seconded cathedral clergy to support the congregation in the village hall, but is unable to find sufficient grounds to sack the vicar.

The clergy live with the dissonance between their two incompatible roles. A minority knowingly neglect their congregations and prioritise their establishment role, fulfilling their public duties from a base in an emptying church. The majority realise that in contemporary society it is building up the distinctive congregation that creates a meaningful and continuing Christian presence. Unfortunately the law of the land and the culture both work against them, requiring them to carry on with those establishment rituals week after week and year after year. They struggle on valiantly, hoping those rituals will draw people into the life of the congregation. When they finally realise such efforts are in vain they fulfil them by rote through fixed smile and gritted teeth.

The tragedy is that those rituals do the church more harm than good. When the church celebrates the Christian marriage of two people who have never been to church before and who have no intention of coming again, or invites a gathering of grinning and distracted parents and godparents and their guests to mouth profound pledges and promises of faith at the christening of an infant who will never come to church again, the church is affirming that they are full members of the church even though they know almost nothing of its life and its faith. It is telling them that this is all there is, that there is nothing more. Far from wooing people into the life of the church, the system assures people that it is absolutely fine to stay away. It mocks the Christian language used in the ceremonies, devaluing its authentic use, it insults those who do attend each week by suggesting that such commitment is worthless and pointless, and it sets up the clergy and their religion as just one more commodity available for a fee, like the children's entertainer at the post-christening party or the chimney sweep booked to attend the wedding to bring good luck.

The work becomes soul-destroying. Those who attend gain nothing, but the church is mocked. The net result is negative: these events do not 'show off the church in a good light': they feature one vicar in one building at an event entirely disconnected from the life of the church. They do not represent the church 'welcoming' those who come: they represent the church as an empty building and a vicar available for hire, for use as the hirers wish. Refusing to host these events would not mean 'turning people away from the church', for they do not come seeking the church: they come seeking the shrine and the shrine keeper and they want nothing to do with the congregation or its strange life and beliefs. Inviting people to join the congregation this Sunday, next Sunday, the Sunday after that, talking to them if they wish about what it all means and why: this would not be turning people away. I longed for the privilege enjoyed by Roman Catholic priests to say, 'We haven't seen you at mass for a while,' or that of free church ministers to talk of regular attendance leading to membership first, but the law of the land said I had to go ahead regardless and they knew it. Those who have actually joined a church through any of these events would have found one by some other means in time. The rest see only a mockery of church: just enough reasons to continue to stay away.

They book their weddings eighteen months in advance. By the time they phone the vicarage they have already fixed the date as they have booked the reception first: a simple matter of priorities. She has always dreamed of a church wedding, he is not really bothered; neither of them has ever been to church. They will not come to church before the wedding and they will not come afterwards either. We tell them it is traditional to attend the Sunday service three times in the final weeks before the wedding, when their forthcoming marriage is announced in church as part of the legal process. They might make it once. You have to make the announcement at the end of the service: if you make it at the beginning, they spend the entire service glancing at the door, looking for a chance to escape.

Most are polite but they want none of that religion. As a general rule of thumb the more money they spend on the day the worse it will be. At the extreme they arrive by heli-copter (there was a patch of level ground opposite the church). The guests are draped in oversized jewellery and refuse to look you in the eye. I have watched guests in the front rows chatter right through the vows. They ask to 'hire the church for the day' and expect the vicar to move at their command. They lay down the law with the cake maker, the dressmaker, the hotelier and the car hire, and they lay down the law with the vicar as well. Throughout the process they mostly despise the cake maker, the dressmaker, the hotelier and the car hire, and they despise the vicar as well: the vicar in particular makes unreasonable arbitrary demands upon them beyond what they have requested and paid for.

Christenings are worse. The committed laity eventually rebel if christenings are held during the main Sunday serv-ice: they are an insult to all they hold dear. At the worst I shouted the entire service over the chattering of two hun-dred adults, wondering at what point they would stop chattering and realise the service proper had begun. They chatted right through to the end. I have watched an embar-rassed father carry the infant out of the pub two minutes after the service is supposed to have begun, followed by his rowdy guests several minutes later. And I have choked on those promises so many times: 'Will you draw them by your example into the community of faith, and help them to take their place within the life and worship of Christ's church?' Some clergy suggest this is a self-certification scheme and ask, 'Who are we to judge?' Very well: just don't let the active laity see. In our multi-purpose building I was dependent on help to set up and clear away even for these afternoon events, and eventually I had worked through all our volunteers: they would witness the spectacle once and refuse to come again.

Booking a christening must have been like booking anything else: a visit to the photographer or a new high-tech pram. My heart would sink at the universal opening phrase: 'Oh hello, I wonder if you can help me.' They were never content with the arrangements though we tried a different pattern every year. 'You don't have to go to church to be a Christian', they would say. Are you asking me or telling me? I would wonder. 'We'd like to come but we're very busy.' I wondered whether they expected to quote their credit card number over the phone and have a christening kit delivered in a White Arrow van. Eventually most would jump through the hoops, attending one Sunday service before the event to fill in the forms and another one afterwards to receive the certificate. Perhaps one in a hundred we ever saw again, usually older children for some reason: there was a run of three- to six-year-olds and some of their parents were key members years later. Every year we tried a different programme for hooking them in, from the liberal 'Of course we'll do it' to the long list of hurdles: watch this video, read this booklet, come to this meeting. None of it made any difference. The families loved the services and our fame spread abroad, but they never came again until the next child was ready to be done. I lamented the state of affairs with a Presbyterian minister in Pennsylvania who was similarly afflicted. He did as many as three a year like this, which he thought was terrible. I was doing three a month. Some Church of England clergy do three a week.

The events we held for our own members showed up the emptiness of the rest. The young Sunday Club leader married his sweetheart in our modern multi-purpose building on a Saturday afternoon. I kept admiring how smart it looked on the day. After years of having non-churchgoing wedding couples insist it was too ugly I had started to believe it, though it had never been true. Later two of our own members married in the middle of the ordinary Sunday-morning service, a highlight of the year for us all. And it was a great celebration every time we baptised one of our own, adult or infant or child, someone who had already been with us Sunday by Sunday and would stay with us Sunday by Sunday for years to come.

A new feature was introduced for those Saturday-afternoon weddings when the service was revised in 2000. After asking the couple for their consents the gathered crowd is asked to give its own consent. 'Will you, the families and friends of John and Jane, support and uphold them now and in the years to come?' All respond, 'We will.' I liked it, until I found myself marrying two of our own members during the Sunday-morning service. Then I realised how utterly inappropriate it was, with its assumption that this was not a gathering of the church for a church celebration but a gathering of people who were strangers to the church, the families and friends of two strangers to the church. Even our liturgies now are liturgies for strangers. I have nothing against people having good wholesome weddings, but the superficial involvement of the church is an embarrassment.

Over the last thirty years the General Synod – the

national governing body of the Church of England – has invested many hours debating the question of second marriages: weddings where one or both of the parties has a former spouse still living. The context for the debate is the church's practice of offering a universal service of first weddings to complete strangers with no questions asked, and the debate has been about how far to extend this to second marriages. One newly elected member emerged from the most recent debate marvelling at the synod's complete failure to connect with the life and faith of the active congregations of the contemporary church: 'Discussing whether we should be doing weddings at all, now that would make a worthwhile debate.'

The church in the twenty-first century will not grow by parading its ministers in their robes at private family events attended by a mixture of the indifferent and the resentful, nor by defending its ancient rights, its parochial monopolies and its seats in the House of Lords. All of this does more harm than good. The church will grow by gathering in congregations that grow together as faith communities that others long to join: communities of prayer, learning and openness, care for one another and for those in need; communities where people flourish in all that it is to be fully human, to be fully alive. Word gets out. People bring people. They say, 'Come and see.'

There is a saying that whenever two or three clergy are gathered together they will talk about funerals. Many do over a hundred a year, all for strangers. I did a good general-purpose funeral – the family was always grateful – but an appropriate funeral for a modern family includes no mention of heaven, and none of the richness of a committed

Christian faith: they would not understand any of the words or images and there is hardly time to explain. If they had any church connection at all their own minister would be taking the service. So I would use some words of comfort from the scriptures and some comforting prayers, offer three or four sentences of tribute – just enough to bring their own thoughts to the fore – and send them on their way with their chosen piece of easy listening as their final soundtrack. It was kind and appropriate with no strings attached, a kindness like visiting prisoners or tending the sick. I would sit in the clergy waiting room at the crematorium listening to the end of the service immediately preceding and cringe with embarrassment as other clergy extended their increasingly trite tributes for people they had never met – their favourite meals and television programmes, the names of all their pets – then struggled solo through inappropriate hymns, and finally took the opportunity to present their version of the gospel: 'Repent of your sins.'

I cannot resent all those funerals I led – those final acts of kindness – though I would never suggest to a family that they request a minister they do not know. Get a recommendation. Ask the funeral director. And for the future: 'This is not my job.' We should be letting the funeral directors take over the entire operation including the service, staking their reputations on having people on hand who will do it well. For the vast majority the faith and life of the church are irrelevant to the occasion, and what is offered is often embarrassingly bad.

Our Roman Catholic and free church colleagues are free from this establishment focus. Their ministry is about being church first of all. Ask about their ministry and the catholic priest talks first about masses and those who attend them. The free-church minister talks about membership rolls and activities. The Church of England minister gives the population of his parish and the number of weddings, christenings and funerals. One of these three has taken his eye off the ball.

Having given the vicar two incompatible jobs, the Church of England then makes him and his family live in the vicarage. Perhaps having a clergy house next to the church made sense during a thousand years of clerical celibacy. It still makes sense today in a large Roman Catholic parish with several priests. The priests live not alone or in partnership but in community, living and working and praying together, supporting and encouraging one another and continually learning from each other, with one or more housekeepers offering practical support in roles from cook to receptionist. But for the last four hundred years the Church of England has allowed the clergy to marry, and from the beginning they never really thought it through. The support of a spouse should not be undervalued, but it is different from the support of fellow priests engaged in the same work and profession. The support of fellow priests in daily companionship has been lost, to be snatched instead in odd minutes when possible. For a few this is at prayers at the beginning and end of the working day; for the vast majority now working alone, it is once a quarter or less at a formal meeting of local clergy. For all the potential support from the active laity, most clergy – understood in their role as salaried staff – are now condemned to work alone. And when the church allowed the clergy to marry it kept them in the vicarage, the big house next to the church. In previous centuries when wives and children were considered chattels of the master of the house, the clergy wife will have dutifully served her man, and the children will have been seen and not heard. In the new millennium the clergy spouse expects both a healthy marriage and an independent life, and the vicarage is almost certainly incompatible with either. The modern vicar lives at work – and the family is forced to live there too.

The free house can sound like a good deal, but it is usually badly maintained, over-sized and difficult to heat. It comes without carpets or curtains or a kitchen unless the previous occupant happens to have left these behind, and the parish generally regards it as a public building, part of its infrastructure. The main parish office is usually inside the vicarage, encouraging encroachment not only into the vicar's home but into his 'home time': there are no off-duty hours when everybody knows that you live at work. Most active lay people – the regular members of the congregation – will respect the vicar's home life as much as they can. It is the people representing the vicar's counter-productive work who ensure that the whole of every evening and every weekend is working time. The presence of the vicar in the vicarage assures them that they are well within their rights and are really being no trouble at all. When you are doing counter-productive work in anti-social hours with complete strangers, there is not much to choose between leaving the house to go on to their territory or inviting them round on to yours. The concepts of family home and quality time disappear. I soon learned not to answer the phone when there was hot food on the table. I learned to unplug it completely on my one designated rest day per week. It was still intrusive to hear the answering machine click on, and there would still be people at the door.

I only made it into a proper vicarage for my final three years. Before that I was in curate's accommodation, which has all the disadvantages of a vicarage without the one benefit of magnificent size. In Burnley and in Harlow the curate's house had only one downstairs room. For ten years I ate three meals a day in my public office, seven days a week. I moved to the Burnley house straight from a college room: kindly parishioners filled it with old furniture. Previous curates had left carpets behind, shrunken with age, leaving gaps around the walls exposing floorboards and the barbs of all the gripper rods. In a row of identical 1970s houses it was the only one that had not been modernised, still single-glazed and freezing cold. A previous curate's dog had left one corner of the main room carpet sticky, and the smell was worse after I paid to have it cleaned. I put a bookcase over it in the end. When I finally made it into a fine four-bedroom vicarage it was magnificent – after I chose to spend thousands of pounds having every single surface in the house repainted and every carpet replaced: the church authorities had bought it from two heavy smokers; every surface was nicotine yellow, as though the entire house had been dipped. On the day I moved in I could smell the nicotine walking up the drive. I could still smell it on my clothes a year later. The vicarage system robs you of even the simplest dignities of choice.

I can't say for sure whether it would have been a good place to live as well as work. It was one of the best vicarages in six hundred parishes after I had renovated it at my own expense and the church authorities had built an office on the front. It was well away from the church in a quiet cul-de-sac, only a few years old and complete with a tidy garden and a pond, but four years previously – after six years in single-roomed curate's houses – I had bought a little pad in London Docklands as my home and I had been commuting to and fro ever since. I felt no inclination to change the pattern on moving to the vicarage. It gave me somewhere to live that was not my place of work. It gave me ten hours out of twenty-four away from the ringing telephone. I spent three or four nights a week there, and a proper day off once a week. I had no idea that stress levels could fall so far. I was a much better person for it, and a much better clergy person. My appreciative parishioners never guessed in seven years.

The church authorities currently spend a highly inefficient £6,000 a year on each vicarage. If some were sold, the invested capital from each could earn at least as much again. The present clergy salary is about £19,000 a year plus a vicarage, and retirement with nothing. As an experiment, some parishes could be offered on the basis of £31,000 a year and the chance to live in the housing mainstream. I suspect they would be overrun with applications. With the vicarage out of the equation a whole range of other options emerges as well: part-time posts, job-share opportunities, and clergy mixing and matching two or more part-time posts of their own choosing. Most clergy households are double-income households and most of the newly ordained have owned a home before. In a recent survey of clergy retirement plans one region found that 50 per cent of all serving clergy already owned another home elsewhere. The vicarage has become an expensive and damaging inconvenience: a counter-productive project.

There has always been anti-clericalism but the late twentieth century saw a collapse in respect for all the professions. A former undergraduate colleague abandoned medicine not because of the difficult training and the long hours but because of the regular abuse from an increasingly ungrateful public. Hospitals, buses and railway stations now display signs politely asking that patrons do not assault the staff. The clergy suffer with the rest in this loss of public respect, and it is multiplied by the classic causes of anti-clericalism: very few people seriously believe that the medical profession or the railway staff are fundamentally malicious, but plenty of people believe it of organised religion. A survey by the Royal Holloway Hospital found one in eight clergy was physically assaulted, one in five was threatened with physical harm and seven out of ten were verbally abused across a two-year period, some of the highest figures for any profession. Much of this abuse took place in the vicarage.

Over the last fifteen years – through Archbishop George Carey's Decade of Evangelism and beyond – a new internal Church of England fantasy has developed to add to the old one about being the soul of the nation. It is just as untrue, and dissent from it is just as strongly condemned. The talk everywhere is of the church being on the very brink of revival and renewal, if not last year then this year or next. The fantasy is promoted in every new report and project, even as we are surrounded by the evidence of terminal decline. The clergy are bombarded with new models of how to be clergy, redefining the entire role according to the latest fashion: how to be pastor, teacher, enabler, community builder, collaborator, prophet, evangelist. Each new model adds to the sense of bewilderment and inadequacy, as the managerial hierarchy redefines the salaried clergy as local managers of a church of volunteers, and judges them in practice on their ability to bring in the cash.

At one time it would have been possible for vicars to regard these pressures as the sacrifices required of them as clergy, but over the last thirty years the church has begun to ordain increasing numbers of part-time, non-salaried clergy with none of these responsibilities. Inside the church they take on the full role of the clergy, indistinguishable from their salaried colleagues, but outside the church they have no obligation to the general public, no vicarage phone, no counter-productive work in anti-social hours. They go to their own homes at the end of Sunday morning, earn their own living during the week, and generally order their lives as they wish. They have virtually no theological training, just some local night classes and a few weekends away. Bishops love them far more than the salaried clergy because they work wonders for the centralised budget, but they leave the trained professional clergy wondering what ordination and vicarage life are all about.

Those money-saving night classes and correspondence courses are now being used for future full-time salaried clergy as well. There are now more future clergy training part-time on local courses than full-time in colleges, a huge conceptual shift in the standard of training expected from the future representatives of the church.

'The problem is the quality of the clergy.' Some took it on

as a dependable second career in which to count out their days to retirement after a mid-life redundancy. Some came into it because they wanted the autonomy and the authority. Some sought the comforts of their own childhood religion or the quiet life of a museum curator. But most were full of ideals for the future – until the system wore them down. For the sake of the team they uphold the twin fantasies of a place in the soul of the nation and a church on the brink of renewal, but they live with the dissonance between the fantasy and the reality. They are isolated, unsupported, no longer respected, under-trained, ageing and over-burdened, bumping along the bottom of a depression covered by the fixed smile of the evangelical and the deep sigh of the liberal. They are good people failed and worn down by the institution.

We came from thriving churches, so we started out believing in it all. Through the selection and training process we were primed with false optimism. Little did we know what lay ahead. Once we were ordained we did our best to build up our allocated church communities according to the models we knew, but volunteers and resources were always scarce, lay people were often suspicious and cynical, having heard it all before, and establishment obligations were a constant distraction. It was rarely possible to do more than keep the show on the road. There was a tragic process of advancing disillusion year upon year. If you scratch the surface you find the same collapsed morale at every level of the organisation, from parish church to archbishop's palace.

Church Langley Church did not have the burden of an ancient building. We had the benefit of a smart modern building shared with the Community Association: bright, clean, attractive, accessible, warm, comfortable and open throughout the week. Novelty meant we were generously resourced with both local enthusiasm and wider support. Being ecumenical (two or more Christian denominations working together) bought us some latitude in terms of both culture and formal structure. We had the direct support of the old Church of England parish church and the sponsoring Baptist church. The curate's house and then the vicarage were well away from the church building. As the new houses went up around us numerical growth was the norm, adding to the sense that something new was always happening. We put out good publicity. We assembled in the round in our versatile modern building, in a great multi-layered arc, gathered around the scriptures and the altar. We used the best contemporary resources for the liturgy. We sang music we enjoyed, both old and new. We held congregation meetings so that everybody was involved. Morale was high, but this was no simple holiday. The main reason people stop going to church is that they move house, and everyone in this newly built development had that in common. It was a highly mobile, highly secularised, highly materialistic culture of cynical third- and fourth-generation non-churchgoers. We were thirty years ahead of the curve in terms of where society is going, but we built a thriving contemporary congregation all the same.

In an ideal week – free from the establishment duties of wedding administration, christening parties and funerals for strangers – my time would be devoted to the life of the local congregation. The excellence of the Sunday liturgy would be a high priority. If seventy people were going to invest more than an hour each in being there, I had a duty to honour that commitment of almost a hundred hours of other people's time. Longer-term planning for the rest of the church programme would also be a priority: future mid-week study courses, special services for important dates in the church calendar, the quarterly congregation meetings, the monthly meetings of the elected lay leadership team, our close involvement with the Community Association, our public profile through signage, literature and leaflet distribution, and the continuous evolution of the Sunday morning programme over time. Together these projects provided more than enough opportunity to be in regular contact with a whole range of key lay people, and I would regularly check the full membership list to make sure that I was reasonably up to date with everybody's situations, a task shared in particular with the elected lay leadership team.

At college we were given a five-point checklist for our own priorities and the priorities of a church: worship, an ongoing programme of in-house opportunities for exploring the faith in depth, programmes to invite members of the local community into the life of the congregation, pastoral care of the congregation, and service to the local community. The establishment duties of weddings, christenings and funerals were increasingly a distraction from these priorities, increasing in number as the population rose, and increasingly out of sync with the life of the committed congregation.

The establishment image was also a burden: halfway through my time in Church Langley I realised I was wearing the clerical collar less and less, especially during the school holidays. I was fed up of being insulted by stray teenagers in the street and receiving pitying smiles in the supermarket. The collar no longer represented God's presence in the community, or anything much to do with God or me or Church Langley Church at all. It represented a despised and resented institution. I bought myself a smart three-piece suit and a set of ties and wore a cross on my lapel. The public respect was immediate and slightly daunting, just as meaningless as the previous reactions but considerably less depressing.

The increasing burden of establishment duties I could do nothing about. We tried every different way of weaving them into the life of the church but they were just painful and harmful and growing in number. When it was time for a new challenge after eleven years in one place, the Church of England could only offer pillars and pews and establishment duties, and a national culture of increasing managerial control in the service of a creeping fundamentalism. I joined the majority of my theological college contemporaries: I walked away.

CHAPTER 2

Hierarchy:
From the Crown to the Curate

Young clergy of my generation set out believing we were joining a church of congregations, or more specifically, congregations and fellow clergy. Congregations would be made up of churchgoers like us, or like we had been until we went off to theological college: people who were committed to the faith and who shared in the life of a congregation as part of their expression of that faith. The clergy and the bishops would be working for the congregations, linking everything together locally and nationally. Those strangely rigorous oaths of allegiance to the bishop and the queen – sworn in a side room in the final minutes before the ordination service – were surely just an irrelevant quirk of history, part of the baggage of being the national church.

We were wrong. The Church of England is not a church of congregations. The congregations are irrelevant: this ship of state could sail without them. The parish clergy are almost irrelevant: the Church of England is a hierarchy of the state and the parish clergy are the lowest rung of that hierarchy, sworn to allegiance and obedience. All the power that matters in the Church of England comes down from the Crown.

The Church of England has forty-three crown-appointed bishops, each with authority over a geographical area called a diocese. A diocese is about the size of county, with one Church of England cathedral and on average about three hundred parishes and two hundred salaried clergy. Once appointed by the Crown the bishop has indefinite security of tenure, and ultimate authority over every parish and minister in his diocese.

Appointment by the Crown now means appointment by the Prime Minister. Since 1977 a formally constituted church commission – now called the Crown Nominations Commission – has advised the Prime Minister of the day, but the Prime Minister is free to reject any name put forward by the commission. Margaret Thatcher regularly used this power to impose her will on a church that she believed was becoming too sympathetic to a left-wing political agenda.

In order to keep such political wrangling out of the public eye, the commission and its proceedings are obsessively secretive. For years even the dates and locations of its meetings were confidential. The commission has fallen into such disrepute that a recent internal church report on its operations spent more time worrying about who controls the paperwork and the flow of information than addressing such fundamental issues as the phenomenal power of this one small group over the entire national church. The commission invites no applications or expressions of interest and conducts no interviews. The secretaries of the archbishops and of the Prime Minister control all the paperwork. Six representatives from the diocese with the vacancy are now invited to attend, but they are out of their depth and outvoted in a commission that meets right at the point where the church disappears into the state. Everything continues much as it did before the commission was formally constituted. Favoured old boys from school and college days are lined up for dispatch to whichever vacancy arises next. Where there are rival lists of favoured old boys the rival parties are politely given one turn each.

Those favoured old boys become the forty-three members of the House of Bishops, twenty-six of whom sit in the House of Lords. Five are regarded as the most senior: Canterbury, York, London, Durham and Winchester. For hundreds of years the culture has been that of a privileged gentleman's club. The camaraderie of royal patronage and autonomous power combined with the etiquette of the English elite to smooth over all differences in theology and practice – until 2003. In summer 2003, nine of the forty-three publicly challenged the Archbishop of Canterbury and the Crown over the appointment of a gay man – Jeffrey John – as Bishop of Reading, even after extracting a promise of celibacy from the candidate. The peaceful privileged atmosphere of centuries was broken, and has not returned.

Every minister in the Church of England operates under licence from one of the forty-three diocesan bishops. Many of those licences are time-limited; and any licence, with or without an expiry date, can be withdrawn without notice. On the day a licence is withdrawn or expires the former licence holder, in the case of the salaried clergy, is immediately both homeless and jobless. The English courts have repeatedly ruled that Church of England clergy affected in this way have no legal redress: they are not protected by employment law. The bishop represents both God and the monarch, and the law and the courts will not interfere.

Licences are occasionally withdrawn and are routinely allowed to expire. The assumption is that if the bishop himself has no new post to offer there will be a post available somewhere else, in some other diocese. Those who do not find one – and do not leave quietly – are routinely evicted. At one stage every curate in my post-ordination training group was facing redundancy and homelessness as the end of our fixed-term licences approached. Posts were being reduced for financial reasons and were therefore scarce, and our existing posts and homes had already been allocated to the next round of new ordinations. There are more clergy left unwillingly unemployed and homeless than the church would care to admit. The two hundred clergy who leave the payroll without drawing their pension each year are assumed to be contentedly working elsewhere, but nobody asks and no records are kept. Ultimately it is the diocesan bishop alone who decides who will have a licence, a salary and a home, and who will not. This is the power of the forty-three diocesan bishops over every salaried minister in the land.

In the absence of even the most basic of employment rights the one check on the absolute power of the bishop is the ancient role of incumbent. Traditionally every parish had an incumbent – more commonly known as the vicar or rector – and like the bishop an incumbent has indefinite security of tenure, known as the freehold. Five thousand of the church's nine thousand salaried clergy are in this position today, although many of them now have responsibility for several parishes, not just the one. By ancient custom every benefice – the post held by an incumbent – has a patron. It is the patron, not the bishop, who appoints the next incumbent when there is a vacancy. The patron's rights date back to the foundation of the parish. The patron may be a local landowner or title holder, or the present vicar of the mother church that established the new parish many years ago, or even a private individual who bequeaths the right of patronage in their will from one generation to the next. Some patronages are held by Oxford and Cambridge colleges as former landowners and benefactors; some are held by the Crown; some have been passed to specially constituted patronage trusts; and over the years many have ended up in the hands of the bishops.

Even beneficed clergy eventually move or retire. At that point a hundred years ago, power would have passed directly to the patron, but now it passes to the bishop: the bishops have acquired the right to suspend any benefice that falls vacant should they so choose. This sidesteps the anomalous power of the patron and hands the power to the bishop instead. The bishop may offer the parish temporary non-beneficed clergy of his own choosing and under his own direct control, or no clergy at all. Some of the Church of England's four thousand non-beneficed clergy are working in these suspended benefices. Others work as assistant clergy – traditionally known as curates – where they are directly answerable to their beneficed incumbents as well as the diocesan bishop. Others are working in parishes where the benefice has effectively been abolished, as in some of the so-called team parishes established since the 1960s.

The contrast in employment rights could hardly be more

extreme between the beneficed with indefinite security of tenure, and the non-beneficed with no employment rights at all. Eventually, in 2001, the European courts determined that the situation was unjust. The church rushed through a consultation exercise to make its response within weeks. I put it to the local clergy meeting that the simplest solution was a standard best practice employment contract. The other beneficed clergy present bristled with indignation at the suggestion that their security of tenure might be compromised in any way, and muttered about the illegality of retrospective legislation. Presumably none of them had the confidence to believe that their bishops or parishes would keep them in post if given half a chance to dismiss them.

The additional powers now held by the bishops are too numerous for the forty-three to manage effectively alone, so intermediate levels of hierarchy have emerged. Most diocesan bishops appoint a small number of assistant, suffragan or area bishops to work under their authority within their diocese. They are appointed directly by the diocesan bishop with the assent of the archbishop and the Crown. They also appoint archdeacons as slightly more lowly assistants, each overseeing an archdeaconry of about a hundred parishes. The archdeaneries are divided into deaneries of a dozen or more parishes. The parish clergy of each deanery meet together regularly as deanery chapter, chaired by one of their own number appointed by the diocesan bishop to act as rural dean or area dean. All these layers of intermediate hierarchy are under the direct control of the diocesan bishop, so everyone knows their place.

Even within the deanery, an informal hierarchy of parishes and clergy emerges. In every deanery in the land there is a subtle pecking order worked out in every detail: beneficed clergy above non-beneficed clergy, ancient parishes above Victorian parishes, Victorian parishes above modern parishes, larger parishes above smaller parishes, distinctive parishes above middle-of-the-road parishes, growing churches above stable churches, stable churches above declining churches, salaried clergy above non-salaried clergy, male before female, and age more important than number of years ordained. Even before we were ordained we had been inducted into this all-pervasive culture. We saw our future ministries in terms of working our way up through this hierarchy of parishes and posts, beginning with three years as a junior curate, then taking one or two slightly more senior non-beneficed posts before a first incumbency in a small and humble parish on the way to greater things, perhaps eventually a fine senior incumbency in a large and ancient parish with a salaried curate and a stint as rural dean. There was no point dreaming of being an archdeacon or a bishop: to ascend that far you need all the right connections long before you are ever ordained.

We had no idea how stifling and oppressive that hierarchy would become. Only rarely is authority exercised directly on threat of dismissal: it is the culture that perpetually oppresses; the existence of a pecking order instead of a supportive collegiality, the presumptive and dismissive criticism from colleagues presuming seniority in that order, and a culture where everyone feels powerless and judged, then takes advantage where they can.

Perhaps there was a time when the culture and structure mattered less, when it was all administered benignly, as we had imagined, for the sake of the congregations of the church. If so that time has gone. In an organisation now riven by internal dispute, the power structures matter at every level from the national to the local, as liberal and fundamentalist do battle for control of what remains of the ancient Church of England.

PART II

History

CHAPTER 3

The Emergence of the Three-Party Church: From the Reformation to the Twentieth Century

When two parties seek to exert influence within a single organisation there is a straightforward push and pull, as the balance shifts first one way then the other. There is little motivation for compromise or creativity and the battle can be bloody. With three parties the dynamics are far more complex and can even be creative. Each party can wax and wane by phases without unsettling the whole, each can learn from the others as they all coexist, creative interaction can take place in relative safety, and the entire operation can flourish as a result.

For centuries a three-party dynamic was the unique glory of the Church of England. It had its 'high church' catholic influences, its 'low church' protestant influences, and its 'broad church' centrist or liberal influences. There was peaceful coexistence and interaction – even mutual appreciation – but the Church of England did not begin that way, and it is not ending that way. It began as a direct two-party confrontation between catholic and protestant, and it is ending as a direct two-party confrontation between liberal and fundamentalist. It is unlikely now that royal or parliamentary patronage will take control to impose a solution, as it did in the sixteenth century, so this time the institution will destroy itself – unless it can find a solution of its own to pull itself back from the brink.

The present tensions go back five hundred years to the reformation. Unresolved issues between church and state go back a thousand years before that, to just five hundred years after the resurrection. At the beginning of the third millennium, this burden of history is finally pulling the Church of England apart. Three centuries of three-party coexistence have collapsed over the last twenty years. Most of the high church catholic party has barricaded itself into a corner and lost interest in what happens to the rest, leaving the soft-hearted liberals of the old broad church standing alone to face the aggression of a fundamentalist party determined to seize control of all that remains.

For the first five centuries after the resurrection the geographical focus of the church was the Mediterranean. The great centres of church life and theology included Constantinople (previously Byzantium, now Istanbul in north-west Turkey), Alexandria (on the Mediterranean coast of Egypt), Antioch (on the Mediterranean coast of Turkey), Jerusalem and Rome. This was the era of the great councils of the church, when gatherings of bishops from around the Christian world defined the essentials of the faith – the trinity and the creeds.

The churches of the eastern Mediterranean survive as the Eastern Orthodox churches, but their global influence waned as a dispute arose between Rome and the eastern churches over the precise text of the creed, and as their areas of influence became increasingly dominated by Islam. To follow the line that leads to global Roman Catholicism, the whole of protestant Christianity and the contemporary Church of England, the geographical focus moves to western Europe.

If the first five hundred years of Christian history were dominated by theology, the next thousand were dominated by western European politics. The church in western Europe acquired both wealth and influence, and for the next ten centuries there would be perpetual tension between the church and the various European emperors, kings and princes for control of that wealth and influence. Appointments to positions of power became a key battleground. Popes and bishops tried to control the appointment of emperors, kings and princes; emperors, kings and princes tried to control the appointment of popes and bishops. Many popes were appointed directly by secular powers for their own secular purposes. Some of those appointed had no church background at all. In its darkest days the papacy was just another European centre of power, with its own lands and armies and both allies and enemies in war.

Despite everything, the church was able to survive this period. The self-interest of kings and princes was often served by maintaining at least a public pretence of support for the institution of the church, and internally the church was held together by the theology of the preceding centuries. The period even had its share of saints and holiness: great monastic centres of learning, significant scholars, and even some holy and reforming popes, the best of whom had usually been monks themselves. There were several extended periods of reform where the church would wrest back control of its own internal appointments from the various secular powers. This required all the power and influence of the papacy. The power of the papacy was originally held not so much over the church as for the church, against secular emperors and kings.

This churning of western European politics dominated the life of the church for ten centuries. The era was brought to an end not by any army or shift in the balance of secular powers but by the spread of a single revolutionary idea in theology: the idea that you could have Christianity without allegiance to Rome.

By the early sixteenth century the church was in great need of another period of reform. Popes were little more than territorial Italian princes and all manner of papal powers – from church appointments to indulgences (special declarations of forgiveness) – were up for sale. Within half a century the entire political scene in Europe would have changed, with the emergence of the protestant churches, and reform in the Roman church as well, through the period known as the reformation.

For Martin Luther – monk, priest and university lecturer – the sale of indulgences was not just an example of internal church corruption, it was the public proclamation of a false theology. The sale of indulgences became the focus for a theological idea Luther had been developing for a decade: that no matter how hard you try you cannot earn, much less buy, your salvation; every individual has done wrong and no amount of good works or personal striving can ever put that right; it is only by God's grace that any individual can be forgiven, and that grace is received by faith, not by any amount of good works.

This material is all drawn from the writings of Saint Paul in the New Testament. Today, for catholics and protestants alike, to set up 'salvation by works' in opposition to 'salvation by grace through faith' is to create a false dichotomy. There may be an apologetic difference of emphasis – as if to justify the history – but catholics and protestants alike believe that forgiveness is a free gift from God that cannot be earned, and that all Christian people should seek to do good. As a doctrine dividing Luther from the corrupt church of the early sixteenth century it was very much a live issue. The church hierarchy was acting as broker of human salvation for its own financial and political purposes, presuming to declare the good works (or fees) required of various individuals in order that they might earn or retain salvation for themselves and for their deceased relatives. The doctrine of salvation by faith and not by works cut right across that brokerage, and right across every possible demand of the church hierarchy.

Martin Luther launched his theological case against the sale of indulgences at Wittenberg in 1517. By the time Rome issued a robust condemnation of his work in 1520 Luther had key supporters in the region, including his fellow theologians at the University of Wittenberg and its founder Frederick of Saxony. Under their protection, and many days' travel from Rome, Luther's theology and its associated reforms were able to take hold in the area. In the Augsburg Confession of 1530 the region set out in detail the terms of its religion. In twenty-one articles they affirmed their adherence to the classic and essential doctrines of the church, condemning named heresies along the way for their own additional protection. In a further seven articles they set out their syllabus of reforms, in every case asserting their conformity to ancient precedent and biblical mandate. These reforms become the protestant agenda: changes to the celebration of the mass, including the practice of having the laity receive the wine as well as the bread; marriage for the clergy; the reform of the practice of confession; a renunciation of monasticism and fasting; and the assertion that valid Christian ministry needs no authorisation from Rome.

For ten centuries emperors, kings and princes had paid homage to Rome for the sake of the Christian faith and the church. Now a major theological movement was declaring that the faith and the church could exist without allegiance to Rome. The details of Luther's theology of salvation were of little interest to the secular rulers of Europe, but the idea that the church and the Christian faith could be retained with or without allegiance to Rome – and that Rome could even be declared the enemy of the faith – would revolutionise the power structures of Europe over the next two hundred years. From here on the reformation would owe more to secular politics than to Christian theology. It presented the opportunity for a complete reordering of Europe's political alliances and enmities without any special regard for Rome. Either alliance with Rome or complete enmity with Rome could equally be presented to the people as a defence of the one true faith. Even where monarchs remained nominally catholic and loyal to Rome – as in France and Spain – they did so entirely on their own terms in a token alliance convenient to both parties. The secular rulers had won the battle for control of the wealth and influence of the church, and even of the religion itself, not with any army but with the convenience of a new theology.

In England Henry VIII took the opportunity to divorce Catherine of Aragon in 1533 in defiance of the pope, dissolved the monasteries – taking control of their substantial assets – and took the title Supreme Head of the Church of England, but overall Henry's English reformation was piecemeal and inconclusive: he was able on the same day to hang three catholics as traitors and to burn three Lutherans as heretics. It was the three monarchs following Henry – his one son and his two daughters – who would define the shape of the English reformation and ultimately the contemporary Church of England.

The child king Edward VI was the son of Jane Seymour, who had died of post-natal complications twelve days after his birth. Edward's six-year reign was managed by the protestant Seymour family, who manoeuvred themselves into the strongest positions at the palace in the final days of Henry's terminal illness in 1547. The first English-language service book – the Book of Common Prayer of 1549 – contained much Lutheran theology. The second edition in 1552 went further, sympathetic to the more strident theology of later reformers like John Calvin. These reforms were not to last. In 1553 the child king died, aged just sixteen, and after the nine-day reign of Edward's nominee, Lady Jane Grey, the throne passed in accordance with Henry's will to Henry's first daughter, the resolutely Roman Catholic Mary, daughter of the rejected Catherine of Aragon.

Under Mary the English church was returned to direct Roman jurisdiction. The Latin Mass was reimposed and all the reforming laws of Henry and Edward were repealed.

Hundreds of protestants were executed, including Thomas Cranmer, Archbishop of Canterbury under Henry and Edward and author of the two editions of the Book of Common Prayer. Some welcomed the return to familiar ways. Others, who witnessed the atrocities, discovered in Mary's short and brutal reign a new repulsion towards catholicism.

Mary died in 1558, just five years after her accession, and the throne passed to Elizabeth, daughter of Henry's second wife Anne Boleyn. After the contrasting reigns of Edward and Mary in short succession, the imposition of religious uniformity would now be virtually impossible. It is in this context that the contemporary Church of England begins to emerge.

Elizabeth's religion was more that of her father Henry than the extremes of the two reigns immediately preceding. She is said to have shown an interest in the Augsburg Confession of 1530 – now a moderate document by the standards of the advancing continental reformation – but to have considered even that a little extreme. She probably wished like her father for catholicism without Rome, and piecemeal reform.

The bishops appointed by Mary would stand for nothing short of full Romanism and almost all eventually resigned. Protestants exiled during Mary's reign returned from the continent radicalised by the advancing protestant theology of those amongst whom they had taken refuge, and many were subsequently elected to the House of Commons. Elizabeth's 1559 Settlement of Religion was a negotiated compromise between the protestant zeal of the Commons and a more conservative Lords and Crown. Elizabeth would have preferred the reintroduction of the more moderate 1549 Book of Common Prayer, but for the protestant Commons the 1552 book was the only option, having been hallowed by the blood of martyrs under Mary. Elizabeth's moderating alterations included the incorporation of some text from 1549, a church structure that retained bishops, and church decoration and clergy dress restored to resemble that 'in the second year of the reign of Edward VI', that is, immediately before 1549.

This mixture of influences was read as permission for wide diversity. Ministerial dress had already become a recognised symbol of theological sympathies: elaborate for catholics, simplified for protestants. When Elizabeth's nominee Matthew Parker came to be consecrated Archbishop of Canterbury in December 1559 the four consecrating bishops wore three different varieties of liturgical dress. In 1565 Parker was charged with imposing nationwide uniformity in ministerial dress. Some ministers had to be dismissed and there were riots in parts of London. From 1570 onwards scores of Roman Catholics were being executed. By the last decade of the century protestant campaigners were being executed alongside them.

Eventually there emerged a centrist or broad church party between the high church catholic party and the low church protestant party. In 1595 Lord Burghley declared himself proud of the fact that the Thirty-nine Articles of Religion (promulgated in 1562) were ambiguous on certain matters, declaring that there were matters too mysterious for even the Archbishop of Canterbury to understand. Elizabeth supported those who began to argue that it was entirely right to retain ambiguity and even mystery around certain questions, like what actually happens to the bread and wine at holy communion. Richard Hooker proposed the application of reason to religion, and considered the Elizabethan settlement to be supremely reasonable. He defended the Book of Common Prayer as the unsurpassable drawing together of the fruits of all centuries of Christian tradition and understanding. In this three-party Elizabethan church we see the contemporary Church of England emerging, with a high church party that is catholic but not Roman, a low church party that is protestant but necessarily tolerant of certain catholic forms like bishops and ministerial attire, and a centrist or broad church party that positively promotes the meeting of traditions and celebrates even ambiguity and mystery, the future liberals of the Church of England.

The centrist party continued but did not come to dominate, for the high church and low church parties remained faithful each to their own cause. Low church scholars drew Calvinist influence from Scotland and the continent. The high church party asserted that the 'uninterrupted' succession of English bishops placed the Church of England within the catholic tradition, with or without a formal link to Rome. Both parties exerted their pressure on the ambiguous Church of England, convinced that things could go their way, but during the reign of Elizabeth there would be no movement in either direction from the 1559 settlement, and Elizabeth would reign for forty-five years through to 1603.

James VI of Scotland (great-great-grandson of Henry VII) was also James I of England from 1603. His son Charles I was king from 1625. They respectively encouraged and enforced a drift towards the Laudian high church (William Laud was Archbishop of Canterbury from 1633). With parliament still suspicious of the catholic cause religion became a factor in the English Civil War from 1642, with the low church parliament fighting the high church king. The king was executed in 1649 and the republic or commonwealth was declared. In Cromwell's commonwealth there was full liberty for all forms of protestant religion. The only requirements placed on the clergy were belief in the trinity and the rejection of bishops, seen as dangerously catholic, papist and Romanist. Cromwell lived only nine years from the declaration of the commonwealth, which collapsed within two years of his death. Parliament restored both the monarchy and the bishops under a new Archbishop of Canterbury in 1660. The Book of Common Prayer was reimposed on the church in 1662 and made compulsory by the Act of Uniformity, a return to the Elizabethan settlement after the divisions of the Civil War. Charles II, son of Charles I, reigned from 1660 until 1685 but his successor, his brother James II, once again proved the dynasty too catholic for parliament and in the Glorious Revolution of 1688 was replaced by his own daughter Mary and her confidently protestant husband William of Orange, who was also a grandson of Charles I.

The Glorious Revolution established the protestant succession, declaring that no Roman Catholic could hold the English throne. For the sake of William's more thoroughgoing continental protestantism it also established the first Act of Toleration, allowing protestants to operate outside the Church of England in their own non-conformist free churches. It would be another hundred years before the beginning of Roman Catholic emancipation, but that one final development would complete the entire English church scene as we know it today: a Church of England established by law as the official religion of the land with high church, low church and broad church parties, and toleration both for independent protestant denominations and eventually for a separately organised Roman Catholic church directly loyal to Rome. The underlying principle of the Glorious Revolution – that a monarch can reign only with the consent of the people expressed in parliament – ensured that subsequent monarchs quietly maintained this religious settlement to the present day.

The church based in Rome did not stand still after 1530 (the year of the Lutheran Augsburg Confession). The objections of the first protestant reformers were finally addressed seriously at the great reforming Council of Trent from 1545 to 1563 (from before the death of Henry VIII in 1547 to after the Elizabethan settlement of 1559). Corruption and abuses were rooted out, but the council made a strong defence of the catholic theology of the sacraments – the idea that God can be present in tangible forms like bread and wine and specific Christian actions. The protestant movement was downgrading the concept, fearing superstition, idolatry and salvation by works, but catholics then and now remained convinced that the sacramental principle is right at the heart of the Christian faith.

Modern catholic teaching presents all world religions sympathetically as responses of the human spirit to the wonder of the created world. Catholicism itself is then defined by faith in Jesus of Nazareth as God amongst us. This is the central claim of the Christian faith: that God took human flesh to walk on earth as Jesus the Christ. It is the concept known as the incarnation, and for catholics the incarnation is not an episode lost in history but a daily reality in the sacraments. In broken bread and poured out wine, in the waters of baptism, in oil for anointing, in marriage, in the ordering of the church through confirmation and ordination and in the declaration of forgiveness by a priest, Christ is made truly present once again to lead us on towards the riches of God's grace. For catholics the sacraments represent the contemporary power of the incarnation, and to deny the sacramental principle is to deny the power of the incarnation. Popular catholic culture happily extends the sacramental principle to include candles, incense, bells, processions, statues, paintings, church decoration, palms on Palm Sunday, ashes on Ash Wednesday, medallions of the saints and rosary beads for Mary, all rejected by the protestant reformers as superstition, idolatry and salvation by works. Many reformers rejected the sacraments altogether, or retained just baptism and the Lord's Supper as outward and visible signs of something inward and spiritual. For catholics this was an assault on the very heart of the faith.

This divergence over the sacramental principle makes catholic and protestant churches look different inside, maintain a different ethos and follow different programmes through the year. In Roman Catholic churches and the high Church of England the main service every Sunday will be the mass, often renamed the eucharist in the high Church of England in deference to Church of England law and sensitivities. There may also be statues, a place to light candles, elaborate formal decoration and colour, a daily mass throughout the week, careful observance of the church year defined by the major church festivals and seasons, respect for the bishop, reverence for the consecrated bread and wine and a priest that everyone calls Father. In the low Church of England and in the independent protestant denominations you find the interior of the building deliberately plain, minimal ceremony, holy communion as the main service once or twice a month or less, vicars and curates and ministers known by abbreviated versions of their Christian names and a church year defined by school terms and calendar months. The broad or centrist Church of England spreads itself out self-consciously between the two.

The 1662 settlement of religion survived the Glorious Revolution of 1688. The next major challenge to the settlement was a protestant revival within the Church of England from 1729 onwards, the Wesleyan protestant evangelical revival. In the end the Church of England settlement could not contain it and the Methodist churches were spawned. The next challenge was a nineteenth-century anglo-catholic revival – the Oxford Movement – celebrating and reviving the catholic heritage of the church from 1833 onwards. There were prosecutions of Church of England clergy for the use of catholic rituals. Some leaders of the movement left the Church of England for the Roman Catholic church, by now much strengthened numerically in England by Irish immigration. Many more stayed in the Church of England, and across the turn of the century became the majority influence in the first attempt at a new Book of Common Prayer since 1662. Approved by large majorities in the convocations of clergy, the Church Assembly and the House of Lords, the book was rejected in December 1927 by the

House of Commons, essentially for being too catholic. It was revised and presented again to the Commons in 1928 – and rejected again, prompting a constitutional crisis: in 1929 the Archbishop of Canterbury declared that 'in the present emergency' the bishops could not regard use of the new material – technically illegal under English law – 'as inconsistent with loyalty to the principles of the Church of England'. The nature of the relationship between church and state had been raised at the highest level in the church with the bold suggestion of civil disobedience in support of the right of the church to govern its own affairs, and to become more catholic than the protestant Commons preferred. There was serious discussion within the church about pressing for a complete separation of church and state, but others argued that sharing in the power and influence of the state was a benefit worth the compromise. The compromise was a new form of internal government for the church that finally came into operation right at the end of the 1960s, fully forty years after the prayer book crisis. The Church of England's new General Synod was not given the right to revise or replace the 1662 Book of Common Prayer, which remains the definitive text to this day, but was permitted to authorise alternative texts for optional use in parishes in place of the equivalent 1662 services. Other matters would still be presented to the Commons and the Lords for approval or rejection. The Church of England remains the established church of the land to this day, with its legislation debated by Parliament, its senior clergy in the House of Lords, and its bishops appointed by the Crown.

CHAPTER 4

The Rise of Evangelicalism

In Europe the theology of the reformation continued to develop beyond the Augsburg Confession of 1530. With Rome removed from the equation, one key question was where to place authority. In England the monarch replaced the Pope. In Calvin's Geneva the city council replaced the pope. In other places churches reorganised into voluntary associations of congregations and ministers as presbyterians, or trusted in the local church alone as congregationalists.

Evangelicalism is the final logical outworking of this devolution and democratisation. In evangelicalism everything comes down to the individual. Protestantism declared that Rome was fallible and that salvation was possible without Rome. Evangelicalism declares that all popes, monarchs, bishops, clergy, councils and congregations alike are fallible and that salvation is possible without any of them, indeed without any church at all. In evangelicalism the salvation once brokered through the church becomes available directly to every individual.

At its best this is a wonderful liberation, an egalitarian revolution. Prince and bishop lose their place as all are declared equal in the sight of God. The fullest riches of God's grace are available to all without distinction. The church exists only as a gathering together of individuals: the individual is primary, the gathering is secondary. Reformation is no longer about the reform and renewal of an international, national, regional or local church: it is about the reform and renewal of individuals one at a time.

This is all consistent with the example presented in the gospels. Jesus calls and challenges people one by one, by name. John the Baptist and the early church baptise people one by one as individual adults, or at most as households, never as whole regions or nations.

Evangelicalism has become the dominant form of protestantism worldwide, especially so in the English-speaking world, and nowhere more so than in the protestant or low church wing of today's Church of England, where its ascendance is complete.

Evangelical theology is fundamentally egalitarian in its assessment of human beings, and yet all is not well. In evangelical theology the king of heaven may be dealing with his subjects directly – rather than through a network of under-lords and barons known as monarchs, popes, bishops and priests – but he is still perceived as a medieval king sitting in judgement on his subjects for the degree of their loyalty or waywardness. Most rank and file evangelicals – clergy and laity alike – perceive their king as generous and merciful. Their theology and their more senior leaders do not.

The Evangelical Alliance is the main representative body for evangelicalism in the UK, across the low church Church of England and the protestant free churches. It aims to 'promote evangelical unity', 'represent evangelical concern' and 'change society'. It has an eleven point Basis of Faith that summarises the essentials of evangelical theology. At the heart of it is the idea that every human being is 'corrupted by sin', which incurs 'divine wrath and judgement', resulting in 'eternal condemnation'. Salvation is won from this wrathful and condemning God by human sacrifice, specifically the sacrifice of God's own Son who has taken human form for the purpose: this is 'the atoning sacrifice of Christ on the cross, dying in our place, paying the price of sin and defeating evil, so reconciling us with God'.

The arrangement can be made to sound generous: God and Jesus come up with a plan whereby humankind can be forgiven; the price of the project is the death of Jesus on the cross; Jesus willingly pays the price. In reality the plan is hideous: God is wrathful and condemning, requires the shedding of blood to assuage his wrath, and arbitrarily accepts the slaughter of his own son as the price for setting aside his judgement. Even this is sufficient to save only one small fraction of the human race.

The entire theory depends on a hopelessly strained reading of a handful of scattered New Testament verses. Its real origin is the reformers' image of God as a wrathful and condemning king. Luther recognised that we could not earn forgiveness from such a king by good works or by any other means of our own, but assumed that forgiveness still had to be won. The death of Jesus on the cross, resembling an Old Testament sacrifice, became the process for winning that forgiveness. What the reformers missed, and contemporary evangelicalism stubbornly refuses to contemplate, is the possibility that God might actually be compassionate and forgiving, rather than wrathful and condemning: a much less strained reading of the New Testament – especially the direct accounts of the life of Jesus – can see the entire work of Jesus as a bold announcement of precisely this reality. As Luther and Saint Paul assert, we cannot earn forgiveness by our own efforts. The good news is not that Jesus earned it for us but that it did not need to be earned: it is a free and entirely unwarranted gift of grace from an infinitely gracious and compassionate God. Liberals read the events leading up to the cross as tragic but typical human history. Catholics surround every detail with rich metaphor. Evangelicals reduce it all to a pre-planned cosmic deal to assuage the wrath of a condemning God.

From the time of the reformation onwards, evangelicals have struggled with the question of who is saved and who is not, and how to tell the difference. The central problem is that the saved continue to sin just like the unsaved. The theory of predestination provides one logical solution: it has the saved and the unsaved marked out before they are even born, drawing on the poetic notion in Saint Paul and the Psalms that God's compassion calls and guides us from before we are born. The theory was sufficiently popular in the sixteenth century to merit inclusion in the Thirty-nine Articles of the Church of England. Unfortunately as it solves one problem it creates another, by leaving some people predestined to eternal damnation, so the ascendant theory amongst contemporary evangelicals is the theory of salvation by repentance. It is by repenting of sin that we are saved: not by successfully avoiding all sin, of which we appear incapable, but by deciding at least to attempt to avoid it. Upon this decision salvation depends. By repenting you buy into the deal done by Jesus on the cross. If you fail to repent, you join the lost in eternal condemnation.

With salvation totally dependent upon full and proper repentance, it becomes essential to ensure that every possible sin has been defined, acknowledged and repented. If there is any doubt about whether a particular action or choice is a sin it is better to declare it a sin than to risk the eternal consequences. The inevitable result is a culture instinctively puritan and conservative.

With its individualistic theology, evangelicalism remains suspicious of all church structures and authorities. It exists not as an institution or collection of institutions but only as an informal network of individuals and groups that share the same theology and culture, so its leaders emerge not by election or appointment but by epitomising the prevailing evangelical culture and so winning popular acclaim. As part of that process, those who challenge the prevailing culture are ostracised or denounced, whatever their position in any church or institution. Beginning with a God of wrath and condemnation, requiring full and proper repentance as the price for salvation, and dependent upon popular acclaim for its leadership, evangelicalism becomes a self-perpetuating network of beliefs and leaders and self-righteous but fearful adherents. The very logic of evangelicalism drives it inevitably towards a cultic fundamentalism.

Thankfully most rank and file evangelicals – inside and outside the Church of England – maintain a healthy detachment from the worst of this excess. They try to live good lives. They remember the words of the gospel: 'Judge not, that you be not judged.' They hold on to the comforting and sentimental idea that Jesus died for their sins, without thinking through the logic of what any part of that statement might mean. They leave it to their leaders to defend the indefensible and they wince with embarrassment at the worst of it, hoping not to be put on the spot about whether they agree with the details or the reasoning. They actually experience God as generous and merciful and that – to be literal – is their salvation.

After the eighteenth-century evangelical revival, and the nineteenth-century anglo-catholic revival, the turn of the twentieth century saw a liberal revival, beginning in the universities of protestant northern Germany. Liberal biblical scholarship was a new examination of the content, format and context of the scriptures. Scholars began to identify different categories of literature within the text: saga, legend and myth, hagiography, poetry and parable as well as literal account. They were taking the text more seriously not less – appreciating its nuance and its complexity. Hand in hand with the re-examination of the scriptures came a re-examination of the world around: the new liberal scholarship promoted a growing awareness of other cultures and faiths, and a serious engagement with the sciences, including astronomy, biology, psychology and anthropology.

The broad church centre of the Church of England, by heritage rational, non-partisan and open rather than defensive, was immediately at home with the new liberal theology. The high church party also had many reasons to feel confident rather than threatened: the anglo-catholic revival had been thwarted initially by prosecutions and the prayer book crisis but by the middle of the twentieth century most of its objectives had been met. Virtually every parish in England had Holy Communion – replacing non-sacramental Matins – as the main service of the day every Sunday, colour and candles and decoration had returned, and the Church of England understood itself as the ancient catholic church of the land, continuous from the earliest times, despite the embarrassment of a separate re-established Roman Catholic church in England. The high church party also believed in the authority of the church: if the bishops and scholars were embracing the new theology it was the duty of the church to follow. If there was a reactionary element in anglo-catholicism it was more about obsession with Rome than a direct rejection of the new scholarship.

For the low church party – by now predominantly evangelical – it was a different story. Already feeling embattled on account of the recent high church ascendancy in the Church of England, they were now confronted with additional challenges to so many of their assumptions about the Bible, other religions and the role of the sciences. Evangelicalism would come to define itself in opposition to liberal scholarship and theology, clinging to its sixteenth-century theology of wrath and appeasement as its only hope for salvation.

By the mid-twentieth century the liberal centre of the Church of England had become more catholic, the catholic wing had become more liberal, and the protestant evangelical wing was feeling isolated and separated. A liberal catholic consensus had emerged, with evangelicalism cast into the role of the loyal opposition. At the liberal end of the consensus the liberals were keen to keep everyone on board, even if that meant soft-pedalling on both the liberal and the catholic agendas for the sake of evangelical sensitivities. At the catholic end the catholics looked on magnanimously, convinced that they alone were the guardians of the one true faith on which both the liberals and the protestants ultimately depended, both liberalism and protestantism being derivative versions of the catholic faith and ultimately dependent upon it. More generally in this still-triangular three-party church only the tip of each corner was pulling away. The vast majority dared to appreciate the richness of the whole.

CHAPTER 5

The Charismatic Era:
1960–1983

The years since the middle of the twentieth century have seen phenomenal cultural change. For the churches, the 1960s were the decade of 'Kum Ba Yah', 'Lord of the Dance' and 'The Family of Man'. The Fisher Folk toured the country, encouraging new forms of Christian music and worship. There were new experiments in community living. There were new hymns, new liturgies, and countless new perspectives on the northern carpenter called Jesus. For the Jesus People he was a long-haired wandering traveller, a storyteller calling people to fullness of life. There was a Jesus People festival in my home town in Lancashire with everyone in robes and tie-dyes. Norman Jewison's film version of *Jesus Christ Superstar* in 1973 depicted Jesus and the disciples as hippies living in the desert on a ramshackle bus: it captured perfectly the contemporary mood of exuberance, freedom and joy.

Over on the continent remarkable things were happening in the Roman Catholic church. Pope John XXIII had been appointed in 1958 and was seen initially as a night watch-

man pope, an elderly compromise candidate with a history
of unremarkable but dependable loyalty: the modernisers
and the traditionalists in the electoral college were presumably content to wait a few quiet years and muster their
energies for the next time. Those few quiet years were not
to happen. John XXIII had been studying the history of the
great councils of the church, of which there had been
around twenty at irregular intervals across two thousand
years. Although the exact role of the councils was undefined
they clearly held an authority and significance far greater
than that of any single papacy or papal pronouncement.
John XXIII decided that in the new post-war era it was time
once again to call a council of the church. Only the second
great council to be held in Rome itself, this would be known
as the Second Vatican Council.

The Vatican's conservative bureaucracy did all it could to
dissuade and delay, but the Pope had made his decision. The
entire agenda of church faith and life would be open for discussion: this would be the defining council for the post-war
world. The Vatican bureaucracy prepared draft documents
in advance of the gatherings, and the assembling bishops
rejected every one of them as too conservative. From 1962
to 1965, across four years of autumn gatherings of bishops
from around the world, and in consultation even with the
churches of the reformation, a quiet revolution took place
endorsed by pope and council together that would permanently change the entire church within a generation. The
council's decisions and their implications are still being followed through decade by decade, a process begun by the
cautious Paul VI (who saw through the completion of the
council following the death of John XXIII in 1963) and

continued through the long and distinguished papacy of John Paul II from 1978 to 2005. For ordinary Roman Catholic parishes in England the most obvious change was in the liturgy: by 1975 Latin had disappeared completely and the entire mass was in English for the first time. The service was led with the priest facing the people. Lay people were taking part, reading scriptures and leading prayers. For the first time catholics were even permitted to share certain services with protestants. Thirteen hundred miles from Rome, in small-town Lancashire, the catholic cubs and scouts joined everyone else for the Saint George's Day Parade for the first time, and even hosted the concluding service. The culture of the church worldwide would be transformed within a matter of years, more radically than at any time since the reformation.

In the local state-controlled Church of England the resentments of the 1928 prayer book crisis were finally being laid to rest. The 1928 services were lightly revised once again and finally introduced as the first series of official alternative services in 1966. The language was still archaic – all 'thee' and 'thou' and 'canst' and 'wouldst' – but the significance was in the achievement of any change at all, the first since 1662. Synodical government arrived in 1970 – internal government at last for the Church of England, still answerable to Parliament but empowered to act alone in the authorisation of further alternative services. The first modern-language services were introduced just three years later as Alternative Services Series Three, and the parishes embraced them. By the end of the decade the church had produced a complete book of alternative services that was to mark decisively the end of the old era and the beginning of the new: the Alternative Service Book 1980.

In ASB 1980 the entire liturgy of the church was in a single volume once again, for clergy and laity alike. Legally it was an ad hoc compilation of authorised alternative services, but it was designed, presented and received as a complete replacement for the seventeenth-century Book of Common Prayer. It included the calendar, the readings, holy communion, morning and evening prayer, even baptism, confirmation, marriage and ordination, all in a confident modern vernacular. Hundreds of thousands of copies were bought by the parishes. Gold-edged copies bound in smart white leather were presented at confirmations. Popular editions were bought for use at home. No parish was forced to move from the old to the new but well within a decade virtually every parish had done so. The church united around the volume that declared its new corporate identity. It was the confident high point of the twentieth-century Church of England.

The unsung achievement of ASB was not the excellent contemporary language – a worthily celebrated milestone – but the complete and almost effortless fusion of the best of the catholic and protestant traditions. At the protestant end adult baptism was made normative, affirming the need for individual conversion, with infant baptism presented as a variation from the norm. At the catholic end the new Roman Catholic mass, emerging from the Second Vatican Council, was presented with only the lightest revisions as the new normative Church of England communion service. From the time of the reformation the catholic-and-protestant Church of England has never been more united than it was in the 1980s. Fifty years after the prayer book crisis a liberal catholic intelligentsia was running the hierarchy of the Church of England, the Second Vatican Council was still refreshing and renewing the Roman Catholic church, and the Church of England was the united church of ASB. Anything seemed possible, even challenging the government. A report on the inner cities did just that and caused a major stir. Every parish in the country was called to raise money for an inner-city rescue fund – the Church Urban Fund – and millions of pounds were raised.

This was the era that produced my own generation of candidates for ordination. We believed in the broad united Church of England with all its rich diversity. At Ripon College Cuddesdon in the late 1980s we were aligning ourselves with the heartbeat of the ruling liberal intelligentsia in its finest hour. The author of that report on the inner cities was our vice-principal. The ethos was the continuing renewal of the church in all areas in the spirit of ASB. The daily liturgy was wholesome ASB three times a day, lightly revised in-house: we naturally assumed that we would be the ones to write the next edition anyway. Amongst our own number we knew and understood traditions both anglo-catholic and evangelical, and we knew that the future was neither and both: the future was liberal.

That liberal complacency was about to be challenged. The classic protestant-evangelical movement that the liberals knew and understood was transforming into something they could neither understand nor control. It was to be larger, stronger, more powerful and more influential than protestant evangelicalism had ever been. Within ten years it would be the most influential force in the Church of England. Within twenty it would have taken control.

The Charismatic Era: 1960–1983

From the entirely informal spirit of the Fisher Folk and the Jesus People there had emerged a new independent exploration of what it means to be a follower of Jesus. The gospels became a direct resource book for what it means to be a disciple. The Acts of the Apostles and the writings of Saint Paul became a direct resource book for what it means to be 'filled with the spirit'. The first stirrings of the charismatic movement just caught the very end of the 1960s. In the early 1980s the movement would be at its authentic height.

It will never be possible to write a full objective history of the charismatic movement: most of those who were there at the time have strong motives now for rewriting the history according to their current agenda. Although every town had its own charismatic groups and fellowships, there was no formal organisation and no inclination to keep records. But I was there, and this is what I saw.

It was 1980 and I was thirteen. For a year I had been attending the school Christian Union but had given up on church. My mother heard about a Christian Fellowship made up of young people in their teens and twenties which met in one of the nearby villages, drawing people from a wide area. The son of one of her respectable friends attended. Contact was made and I was invited along, and so I found myself outside our local church after a Sunday-evening service, waiting for the minibus out to a farmhouse near the outlying village of West Bradford.

More people were crammed into one room at the farmhouse than could decently fit, even sitting on the floor: they sat in the doorway and the next room as well. Brian the host and Myrtle his wife were relaxed and happy and part of the group. They perched on tiny infant-school chairs to avoid taking up any more floor space than was absolutely necessary. Everyone had brought their own Bibles. A handful of people had brought guitars.

The evening came in two distinct halves. The second half was fairly conventional teaching for the age-group: introduction, activity, discussion and epilogue, and constant reference to those Bibles with which everybody seemed most confident ('Turn to Galatians chapter 2, verse 20'). It was the first half of the evening that was extraordinary.

I was used to the idea of open prayer from the school Christian Union: we would sit with our eyes closed and between pauses take it in turns to address God. I was used to the idea of open discussion: we would sit with our eyes open and between pauses make small contributions. The first half of the evening in the farmhouse was like both mixed together, on speed and with added guitars.

Before it all began there was a sense of bright anticipation that something wonderful was about to happen. Once it began it had a momentum all of its own. People shared pieces of upbeat news from the week. People read out Bible texts. Others reflected out loud on what had been said, with affirmations and more Bible quotations and snippets of affirming theology. There were songs that everyone knew, and sang and played loudly and confidently. Not even the musicians had songbooks.

'That is God's assurance!' declared Brian brightly, affirming one contribution. 'I've got that blessed assurance,' said someone else after a pause. 'Amen!' hollered Brian with a grin. These people are weird, I thought; and then it turned out all right. The exchange had been a deliberate, gently self-mocking joke. 'I've Got That Blessed Assurance' turned out to be a song. One of the guitarists struck up a chord and the whole gathering began to sing. Most of these choruses had only half a dozen lines, repeated three or four times, so it was easy to join in. In Lancashire at the beginning of the 1980s the Jesus movement of the sixties and seventies had grown into something full of life – very full of life – for this fellowship of young adults, and from that day I was a part of it. Within six months I had my mother's guitar with me, watching the chord sequences of the other guitarists and following along.

Ten years later at theological college, a small group had to choose a new supplementary hymnbook for use in college, and chose *Songs and Hymns of Fellowship*. 'Oh God,' declared one older member: 'the history of the charismatic movement, 1970 to 1985.' He may be right: the several incarnations of *Songs of Fellowship* may be amongst the most significant pieces of documentary evidence surviving for the history and evolution of the charismatic movement. A friend in the fellowship had one of the first editions, with just fifty-three songs. I own the second edition of the title with 135 songs. There was great excitement when Volume 2 came out with 189 more. The 2003 edition has 1,690 songs. Clearly something happened.

The latest edition boasts a list of famous song-writing contributors. In my edition of 135 songs, most of those we knew are credited 'anonymous'. Those early songs were collected like traditional folk songs, not promoted on behalf of famous-named composers. I recently found my old handwritten notes of the songs we used to sing: fewer than half of that collection appear in any printed songbook. They were our songs, shared between fellowships like ours, the melodies remembered, the chords worked out, sung in farmhouses, village chapels and camping barns. It was the tail-end of a true folk movement.

It turned out that Sunday night was just the 'lite' version of the main event. The main event was Friday night in the village Methodist chapel. It was mostly the same group of people but the average age was slightly higher: we gained a few adults and lost the youngest teens. About forty or fifty would gather. They belonged to a whole range of Sunday churches but about half were from Saint James's, technically my own Church of England parish church although I had never been. People brought their Bibles and several brought guitars. The benches of the chapel were rearranged to be less formal.

Like Sunday, it was an evening of two halves. The second half was now a sermon by a visiting speaker. The first half was like Sunday's, but more serious. Open discussion was kept separate as a collection of individual contributions right at the beginning: 'Does anybody have anything to share?' After that the format resembled open prayer: everything was addressed directly to God, nothing was pre-planned, and anyone could contribute. It was the nature of these contributions that made Friday-night fellowship so distinctive.

There was music, there was silence and there was speaking into the silence. The silence was not so much the space between the contributions as their foundation. We were in the presence of God, and silence was appropriate: silence and song, and words spoken humbly.

The style of music became known commercially as 'praise-and-worship', but we knew that praise and worship were different things. Praise was loud, upbeat and triumphant, with people on their feet. Clapping along was for the timid: most went straight to dancing, an energetic vertical bounce, like disco or nightclub dancing but without the erotic swing and sway. It was always clearly optional: people would stand or sit at will, you could do as you pleased. In the gaps between the praise songs everyone would speak at once: 'Praise you, Jesus,' 'Glorify you, Jesus,' and then another would begin. And worship was silent, a silence embraced by beautiful and gentle love songs to Jesus, as soft as lullabies. People would sit with eyes closed or stand with their hands open heavenwards, and time disappeared. No two meetings were alike. The spirit of the evening, or the spirit of the gathering, or perhaps the spirit of God, made each evening unique.

It was the intensity of the quietness of the worship that I found to be the deepest expression of an authentic spirituality: to be a part of the gathering, caught up in silent awe into the very presence of God, hesitant even to breathe except to make another offering of adoration, another expression of love for God.

Occasionally contributions would take one of the forms that made the charismatic movement of the time both distinctive and controversial. We learned what it all meant through experience, through Friday-night preaching, and straight from the New Testament, where Saint Paul writes extensively about similar happenings at Corinth and elsewhere. These were the experiences that put the charism (gift) into charismatic (gifted).

75

Firstly there was prophecy. Someone would start talking like an Old Testament prophet: 'I will be your God and you will be my people . . . I will watch over you and keep you . . . I will lead you onwards into ever greater things . . . the glory of my name will be revealed . . . and many shall come to know that I am the Lord your God . . .' and so on, often for two or three minutes at a time. They were uplifting and encouraging words, sometimes gentle, sometimes more strident, but always very much in the tone of the Old Testament. Sometimes one of the emerging themes of the evening would be reflected in the contribution. We all bought into a theology that said these were direct, specific, live messages from God for those gathered in that place at that moment. In reality they tended to be uncontroversial set-pieces, well constructed and well delivered by people who were good at that sort of thing anyway. Most inserted 'The Lord says' and 'says the Lord' at regular intervals. Only the most confident spoke without these tags as though speaking directly the word of God. Thankfully in our fellowship these contributions were always benign: in other places the abuse of this format has been a great way to cause chaos.

Then there was speaking in tongues. Saint Paul writes about the phenomenon at length, encouraging its use in private prayer and discouraging – but not quite forbidding – its use in public. The sound is like someone speaking a foreign language. Straight from the Acts of the Apostles and Saint Paul, we bought into a theology that saw this as a special gift of the Holy Spirit for the building up of the individual and the community. As in Acts chapter 2 most chose to believe that the sound was that of a real language. Various urban myths spoke of occasions when a message in tongues had been heard and understood by someone present who happened to know the language being spoken. We were also content to believe that the language was sometimes the language of the angels, genuine but unknown on earth. Researching today, I find that the phenomenon is known not only in other religions but in some forms of schizophrenia, and is assumed to be no more than a collection of random syllables to which are added the cadences of speech. This does not worry me at all. There is a certain feeling of letting go about it, and in the context of prayer that is letting go into prayerfulness. It gives you something to do with your voice, just as an icon gives you something to do with your eyes and a rosary gives you something to do with your hands. It is soothing, encouraging and serious all at once. It feels like prayer underlined. Whispered it has a beautiful warmth. Used in public it resembles prophecy, as described above, except that nobody hearing can understand, and the contribution is known as 'a word in tongues'.

A third phenomenon – interpretation – goes with a word in tongues. Alone it would resemble prophecy, as described above, but following a word in tongues it is said to be the same message, repeated in the vernacular. Again the theology comes straight from Saint Paul. If there was no interpretation after a word in tongues there would be a moment's disappointment but it would pass. One regular visiting preacher would always provide an interpretation if nobody else did, and it always seemed rather similar to the previous time he was there.

Visions somehow seemed gentler and more manageable than the uncontrolled exuberance of prophecy, tongues and interpretation. Someone would speak into the silence: 'I've got a vision,' and there would be a description of some scene. Sometimes the meaning of this parable or illustration was obvious. Sometimes the person bringing the vision would explain the meaning. Other times it would be as nonsensical as a bizarre dream and there would be a pause, waiting for someone else to bring the interpretation, a bit of shared amateur dream analysis.

There were other wonderful sounds in those times of praise and worship. Often the song would conclude and a patchwork of other sounds would begin. People would speak out loud all at once – 'Praise to you, Lord,' 'Glory to you, Lord.' A guitarist might strum some chords. Someone might sing a few words rather than speak them. Others might join in, building a spontaneous harmony of voices. Add a few people doing that in tongues and it is called 'singing in the spirit', and has to be one of the most rich, complex, beautiful, spontaneous and joyful sounds on earth. Often in larger gatherings it would rise through different cadences and phrases and include episodes of applause and speech and changes of harmony. Just once I heard it include laughter, like the affectionate laughter of an applauding audience, beautiful, rich, warm and embracing: 'laughing in the spirit'. And the most beautiful sound I ever heard I can hardly describe. Certainly it could not be written in any musical notation. Into the silence one of the musicians began to sing alone, in English or not I do not remember. The sound was ethereal, unearthly, totally beautiful, soaring and swooping, like nothing anyone had ever heard. This went on for a while and people listened in rapt silence. Then across the room another singer began in the same style. The two voices swooped together through awesome harmony and dissonance and resonance for minutes more. And then silence: a beautiful, expectant silence.

The Friday-night fellowship was the latest incarnation of a group that had been meeting in different formats right through the 1970s. Since 1974 there had been an annual camping weekend at the farm. Hundreds of people would gather with tents and caravans for three days of meetings in a great barn in the only month of the year when it was clean and available, just a few weeks before the silage was cut. Rows of seats were created from bales of straw. Cables were suspended across the farmyard, bringing power for light, sound and music. All day there would be different events and gatherings – worship, teaching, prayer, bible study – but the two main events were the Friday- and Saturday-evening meetings, each drawing a further crowd of visitors. These were like the usual Friday meeting but amplified yet again. 'Sharing time' was now a cabaret of performance pieces: bands, drama and testimonies. Praise and worship would run and run, although the sheer numbers meant that those with the microphones and musical instruments had more say than the rest in where it would go next. And late in the evening, after the sermon, came 'ministry time'. On a straightforward night people who wanted to make a commitment would be asked to come to the front. Fellowship members primed in advance would join them to talk them through it as the music continued. On a more complex night the speaker for the evening would lead the ministry time himself, calling people forward for a whole range of different reasons – for healing, for new gifts, for prayer to overcome some personal struggle, for a renewed filling with the spirit – and pray with each of them in turn. This is where on occasions some or many would fall to the ground 'slain in the spirit' and just about anything – a racing heart, shaking, shivering, panicking – could be a 'manifestation' of the spirit. Some ministers would deliver 'a word of knowledge' about some specific need 'in here tonight' and call on the person concerned to join the others for prayer at the front. For a while the music would continue and the whole gathering would be praying for those who had gone forward. Eventually the meeting would break up rather than end – a relaxed conclusion to the whole event – with many staying for hours more to pray or talk while others drifted away.

My favourite contributor to those weekends was a singing nun. She brought her own guitar. She told of finding a book in the convent library about the charismatic movement with the delightful American title *Wow God*. She had gone to ask her mother superior, 'Why aren't these things happening here?' Mother Superior smiled a wry smile and said, 'How do you know they aren't?' She sang: 'Tell my people I love them, tell my people I care; when they feel far away from me, tell my people I am there.'

I lived the whole of my early teens in this vibrant and ever-evolving charismatic Christian subculture. In November 1980 I was baptised by full immersion, alongside three others, in a pool dug in a stream in the hills above the farm, waist deep in water and ankle deep in mud, with Brian the fellowship leader on my left and the minister of the local Pentecostal church on my right. At camp in 1981 I was persuaded to join the music group from Saint James's for some performance pieces, and found myself a weekly member of Saint James's from there on. Later that year we had a wonderful trip to a concert by Sheila Walsh and the Mark Williamson Band. I bought both records. Just before Easter in 1982 we visited Spring Harvest in its fourth year, a larger commercialised version of camp held at Pontin's in Prestatyn. We spent the whole of Good Friday back at the farm, wandering the fells and checking on the lambs. The next year – 1983 – we went to Spring Harvest for the whole week. There is a photograph of me on Prestatyn beach with a beaming smile. It captures the spirit of the time.

Those two old vinyl LPs from 1981 also capture the spirit of the moment, both the excitement of the time and its particular obsessions. Sheila Walsh has some excellent poetic descriptions of the experiences we knew as being 'born again' and being 'filled with the spirit'. 'Never knew that life could be so fine. Never thought that love could change this heart of mine.' 'You're understanding, though you're demanding. I find your love impressive and disarming.' 'Your love has melted my ice into tears.' 'Your presence burns like fire in my soul.' 'Your spirit gave me eyes of a different kind.' She was singing for all those sharing the charismatic experience of faith.

The album also reflects the strange mixture of confidence and paranoia of the time. Everything was seen as a great battle between good and evil, both in the life of the individual and in the frightening world outside. This was long before cheap international travel or instant global communications. International telephone calls were still an unreliable novelty. The Cold War was at its height, making half the planet completely invisible. The internal battles against temptation and worldliness were mapped directly on to global and cosmic battles of good against evil. 'Oh for a voice to chase away the demons of the dark. Oh for a voice to speak in peace into a fearful heart. Oh for the soothing sound of it to chase away the fear of silence.' Addressing the personal paranoia there was the soothing promise of comfort and forgiveness: 'Pouring out forgiveness on a guilty furtive soul.' 'He weeps for our tears and he bows with our pain.' Addressing the global and cosmic paranoia there was the apocalyptic obsession of the time: we believed in an imminent apocalypse, the return of Christ, the definitive moment in the cosmic battle between good and evil, and the ultimate nihilistic relief from all the struggles of the present world. 'I see the end of all the proud affairs of men.' 'The sparkling lights of mighty cities all go out.' 'I hear the roar of heaven's armies march to fight.' 'The time is almost here.'

A whole bizarre theology of the sequence of events then triggered had been popularised during the 1970s – the tribulation, the rapture, the thousand years, a specific sequence of global catastrophes – all following on from the visible signs of its approach: changes in the Middle East, the new global communications satellites, the translation of the New Testament into the last few remaining indigenous languages, technology venturing where only God should go, even the expansion of the European Economic Community and electronic transactions replacing cash. The biblical books of Daniel and Revelation were scoured for clues, along with the apocalyptic words spoken by Jesus himself in Jerusalem just days before the crucifixion. We believed that the final days of God's plan for the world were being played out around us, and that the charismatic movement sweeping the world was essential to that plan.

The Charismatic Era: 1960–1983

In our minds in the early 1980s the whole sequence was thoroughly confused with the Cold War and the accompanying threat of nuclear oblivion. The Cold War itself served as a global last battle for the very soul of the human race, and the threat of nuclear catastrophe matched so much of the detail: its imminence, its inevitability, its unpredictability, its global nature, the ruination of the planet, the survival of the few, the nuclear winter and a thousand years of chaos. The global battle between good and evil became personal through a whole theology of demonology and deliverance. It seemed that any problem at all could be traced to a demon – at times there seemed to be more demons than people. There were warnings about cults that drew gullible young people into the service of charlatan leaders. Some of them had looked quite Christian – even spirit-filled and charismatic – before they went so very wrong, adding evidence to the widespread proposition that the devil is most active 'where God is most active'. We mocked the Jehovah's Witnesses and others for allegedly suggesting dates for the end of the world, but we all nodded sagely when one elderly Friday-night speaker suggested 'before the year 2000'. Add the miners' strike, George Orwell, and rumours of brainwashing, indoctrination camps, acid trips, addictions, mass suicides, false prophets, modern witchcraft, satanic rituals, freemasonry, espionage, the international mafia, astrology, eastern mysticism, the mysteries of hypnosis and depth psychology and the investigation of the paranormal, and you have a seriously paranoid and embattled subculture, for all its claims that God would triumph over everything in the end.

Healing was another major obsession. We believed in

miraculous healing through prayer. It was documented in the bible so we expected it in our own day. Many patterns of prayer for healing emerged, but the most significant was assumed to be prayer with 'the laying on of hands' – placing the palms of the hands on the shoulders or head of the person concerned – especially if the context was the ministry time towards the end of a charismatic meeting, in response to a word of knowledge announced by the evening's main speaker. There was always a handful of stories circulating about healings that had taken place. Mostly it was internal or psychological – there was never much to see – but there was always somebody who knew somebody who had had a major physical ailment miraculously cured. There were increasingly complex theologies – not all of them particularly benign – for explaining why the prayers 'sometimes' did not work. Most of those receiving prayer went away still ill or disabled but with the additional task – or guilty burden – of wondering why it did not happen for them.

Those who went forward for prayer towards the end of a charismatic meeting were ultimately self-selected, even when they were responding to a word of knowledge about a particular need. Just once at camp a visiting speaker roamed around the gathering picking on people at random – telling them by word of knowledge what their deepest problems were, and praying for them out loud in front of everyone. On the evening itself we went with the flow – the music continued, a babble of background voices joined in the prayers – but the next morning the word all over camp was that a member of the local fellowship picked from the crowd the night before was openly disowning what had been said as irrelevant and wrong and therefore not from God at all. At the time we chose not to work through to the logical conclusion of this observation – not out loud anyway – but that particular speaker was not invited again.

Alongside the obsession with healing this is the other major charismatic problem: the problem of faking it. It can look so dramatic and so convincing. You watch the superficial drama and you copy it. You work the crowd to get things going, and bring on a team with the same set of skills. You say all the things people want you to say. You prey on vulnerability and longing. You put on a show.

Years later at theological college a group of students was discussing the phenomenon of the large charismatic meeting and its distinctive elements, like people falling to the floor 'slain in the spirit'. One of the students had a video of a meeting that she kept as evidence, showing part of the ministry time at a charismatic gathering of thousands. The self-selected seekers were lined up side by side at the front, with the speaker's helpers around them. Moving along the line he prayed loudly over each one in turn, always with one hand on their shoulder or their forehead. At a climactic moment he would shout some of the words of his prayer and give a hearty shove. Submitting to the expected pattern, the seeker would stay rigid and fall backwards, to be caught by the helpers and lowered to the ground.

Last year I saw a documentary about stage hypnosis: hypnosis used for entertainment. It described the controversy and fear that now surround the practice, the accusations and the rebuttals. Towards the end they showed the latest class of new recruits learning the basics. The first thing they were taught was how to make somebody fall over backwards completely rigid. You persuade them to stay rigid, put a foot behind their feet and push the shoulder or, better, the head. It was a moment of appalling clarity. A stage hypnotist asks for volunteers. Those who come forward are self-selected. He works with them to find the ones who are most responsive, most suggestible. At the moment of his choice they are slain in the spirit.

Halfway through the 1990s there was a new wave of falling to the floor and showing other 'manifestations of the spirit', mostly quaking and shaking whilst lying on the floor. It was billed as an entirely new phenomenon heralding a whole new era in the work of God in the world. The normally sombre *Church Times* reported it as unprecedented. *The Times* reported it as unprecedented. People who love a bit of supernatural drama declared it unprecedented and worked up into a spin of excitement. Where were they all ten and fifteen years before?

In the 1990s it began at a so-called mega-church in Toronto and spread from there, becoming known internationally as the Toronto Blessing. As it hit one church after another people would say, 'The Toronto Blessing has arrived.' Reports of new developments would fly around the globe. Soon people collapsing on the floor at the affected churches would be 'roaring like a lion'. They could spiritualise that one with a biblical reference to the Lion of Judah. Next they were 'barking like a dog'. At this point I think they just mixed up the letters of Saint Paul in the New Testament with the Beginner's Guide to Stage Hypnosis: 'Everybody bark like a dog.' The whole thing was a textbook case of mass hysteria.

There were people taking these reports seriously in virtually every church in the land, so as a working vicar I was forced to have an opinion. I suspect that, for many of the uptight, stressed-out, middle-class people who go to events of that kind, an hour on the floor shaking or weeping or barking like a dog – or just resting – is probably the most peaceful, relaxing, de-stressing and potentially life-changing experience they are likely to have in a decade: a complete letting-go into a state of prayerful bliss. It is certainly not going to be the most effective or dignified way of addressing their issues, but it was readily available for a while, and quick, and free at the point of delivery. I doubt that its long-term impact on the individuals or the church was entirely benign, however. It would certainly not be helpful to maintain that it was a particularly important work of God for our time.

From my liberal catholic theological college there was a number of college exchanges each year. A group of mostly ex-evangelicals and ex-charismatics did an exchange week with one of the predominantly evangelical-charismatic colleges. While we were there the host college had a designated in-house charismatic event. These people lived on campus and had meetings and services together daily, but this one event was specifically designated the charismatic one and held just once or twice a term. Only college members and we visitors were present. It was in the middle of the day in some functional lino-floored room. All the phenomena were duly displayed right on cue by the students present: people in distress receiving ministry, visions, words of knowledge, prophecy, all of it either hysterical or horribly faked. We came away deeply disturbed.

I realised twenty years ago that the third commandment – 'Do not take the name of the Lord your God in vain' – has very little to do with what you happen to say when you are taken by surprise, and everything to do with those who presume to know the mind of God and to speak in the name of God. It is quite properly higher up the list than a straightforward misdemeanour like adultery, murder or theft. I came to realise that amongst all the apparent gifts – prophecies, visions, interpretations – the only one that really matters is the gift of discernment: discerning a right spirit from an impostor who is taking the name of the Lord in vain. Saint Paul lists the spiritual gift of discernment amongst all the others so it was earnestly discussed, but the logic becomes circular: who can discern who has the gift of discernment?

In what remains of the charismatic movement, market forces now fill this gap. Book sales, well-attended conferences and large congregations become the signs of legitimacy, along with television channels, radio stations, fame, wealth, mutual endorsement and substantial pieces of real estate billed as Christian centres, producing an informal hierarchy of known charismatic leaders locally, nationally and internationally. It loiters on the margins of hero-worship. It hands phenomenal power to those whose stock is high.

Way back at the reformation there was a protestant solution to the problem of discernment: the assurance that everything necessary for salvation was already there in scripture, and anything else you are free to ignore. There is also a catholic solution: that no personal revelation is to be fully trusted until affirmed by the pope, who serves as the final arbiter of all discernment. A decision is usually forthcoming about a hundred years after the event. Saint Paul also offers methods of discernment: for example, you can tell that a prophecy is true if it comes to pass. This somehow robs a prophecy of its immediate impact and significance. And Jesus offers this test for the false prophets 'who come to you in sheep's clothing but inwardly are ravening wolves': 'You shall know them by their fruits.' Now, when considering diverse factions in the church, I find myself asking: Is there love? Is there humility? Is there peace? Is there that mysterious quality that some have called holiness? Is there patience, kindness, faithfulness and gentleness? Or is there instead anger, self-importance, envy, greed, deceit, excess and arrogance?

The West Bradford fellowship was kept on track by a shared humility before God and one another. Humility before God was expressed in reverence and awe at the mystery of God, and in the silence. Humility before one another was experienced as a profound sense of interdependence and community, and ongoing responsibility for one another. Take away that humility and that sense of community, give one person a microphone or a clerical collar or the dream of celebrity, add some sinful human pride, and all you have left is a set of powerful toys to use as you will: for stage hypnosis, or marketing, or building a cult.

Perhaps it was right there at the fifth Spring Harvest in 1983 – nine years after the first West Bradford camp – that the charismatic movement simultaneously came of age and lost its innocence of youth. The larger charismatic gatherings were becoming less folksy and more focused on key national figures. Worship was no longer spontaneous and shared but led entirely from the front by people with microphones. Commercial elements were moving in. Main-stream evangelicalism was claiming the movement as its own. Classic evangelical dogma was taking over from 'the freedom of the spirit'. The charismatic movement as an authentic folk movement of the sixties and seventies had run its course; something altogether different was emerging, claiming for itself both the name and the heritage. Twenty years later its power and influence control the national church at every turn.

By 1980 all the salaried staff of the Church of England knew about the charismatic movement. Every town had its own charismatic groups and fellowships, so all the local clergy knew. Many – including archdeacons and bishops – were beginning to meet people influenced by the move-ment. Amongst those influenced were many who also belonged to Church of England churches, including some already ordained and others now coming forward for ordination. An official report on the movement was com-missioned by the General Synod in 1978 and completed in 1981 by Church of England charismatic insiders. It was for the most part helpfully objective on the state of the move-ment at that particular moment in time, but everything has changed since then. The charismatic-evangelical merger took place about 1983.

The early charismatic movement was not a place of evan-gelical dogma – it was a place of authentic experience shared – but by the early 1980s it was looking for a frame-work, an established language, a reference point, even a respectability. Mainstream evangelicalism, with a cultural and theological heritage going right back to the refor-mation, had initially been deeply suspicious of the new charismatic movement. Some influences had worked their way through into evangelical culture – open prayer, discussion groups, some of the music – but the 'supernatural' phenomena had been thought too dangerous by far. For its part the charismatic movement had understood itself as entirely new, and was deeply suspicious of anything with a history.

Nevertheless each side began to see potential benefits in building bridges. Authors, speakers and commentators in each movement led the way, at first merely noting similarities, then speaking positively about them. Soon a fairly confident alliance was emerging. Within a few years any clear boundaries between evangelical and charismatic would be gone, and the two movements would have completed the merger that would dominate protestant Christianity in Britain for decades to come. Within the combined movement there are still those who prefer one term over the other, but in the new century charismatic and evangelical belong to a single clan.

For the charismatic movement the merger offered a ready-made theological framework and a share in the practical inheritance of many decades: organisations, publications, networks, endowments, whole libraries of thought and opinion, established terms of reference, a certain respectability, and a weight of theology to begin to deal with the torment of all those failed healings and perhaps to discern the wholesome from the fake. For the grand old evangelical movement the merger offered a major injection of new energy. It brought new life and vitality into a dusty old building, changing the atmosphere of the place but saving it from simply crumbling away. It also neatly removed the threat posed by an upstart rival, capturing all that new energy for the continuation of its own heritage instead.

Tragically the most significant problems of both parties are retained through the merger. The combined charismatic-evangelical movement retains as its God the wrathful medieval king who condemns you on account of your sins, the direct route into fundamentalism. It retains an obsession with healing. Its love of spiritual drama and its individual-istic culture push its heroes and its wannabes deep into the temptation towards fakery. The extempore in prayer and preaching is assumed to be more spiritual than the pre-pared. Divine authority is claimed for visions, prophecies and other messages from God. There is an obsession with the dramatic, from speaking in tongues and being 'slain in the spirit' to demonology and exorcism. And the whole movement lurches recklessly into whatever looks exciting and new for the sake of 'reaching out to the current gener-ation': sixteenth-century theology in a baseball cap. It is a tragic end to the authentic spiritual revival of the 1960s.

The most wholesome aspects of protestant spirituality were lost in the merger: its calm and gracious confidence in the Rock of Ages, its uncomplicated faith in the all-suffi-ciency of scripture, its egalitarian spirit asserting that the fullness of God's grace is available to all without distinction, and its political heritage in the abolition of slavery and the origins of the Labour movement. Lost also was the best of the early charismatic movement, when there was silence, wonder, reverence and awe at the mystery of God, when the anticipation was genuine rather than demanding, when the published songs were anonymous collected folk songs, when the music, prayer and sharing were led from within the group not from the front, and when the charismatic phenomena were spontaneous and shared, not delivered on cue at specified events like the Alpha Course's Holy Spirit Day. In those early days, the space for welcoming something new was for experiencing God, not for marketing and rebranding. The laughter was exhilarating, not a cover for embarrassment. Humility and a sense of community saved the movement from folly and excess: the movement used to listen to its members rather than judge them; sharing authentic experience was more important than falling into line; and a singing nun could smile a wry smile and have the entire gathering hanging on her every word.

Soon after that fifth Spring Harvest in 1983 the leaders of the West Bradford fellowship decided that after six and a half years the Friday-night meeting had run its course. It closed that September. Half of the fellowship focused their allegiance back at Saint James's, where a new charismatic rector was in post. Most of the other half formed a new independent church several months later. The rector and the music group at Saint James's tried to make Sunday service more like Friday-night fellowship – vainly imagining that music was the key – but the Friday-night experience would not survive the transition to Sunday morning at either Saint James's or the new church. Its moment had gone.

CHAPTER 6

Descent into Chaos: 1983–2005

A wise archdeacon once suggested that you can learn almost everything you need to know about a church by observing its liturgy. Is it dominated by one person, or is it a genuinely corporate event? Is the singing bored and functional, or confident and sincere? Are the clergy treating the laity like children, or like adults? Are people participating in the liturgy with all that they are, or just reading it from a book or a sheet and doing as they are told? Is it awkward or wholesome, a chore or a privilege, a habit or an unmissable event?

The Church of England is a church defined by its liturgy. The seventeenth-century Book of Common Prayer defined the Church of England from 1662 to 1980. In 1980 the church embraced its new self-definition in ASB. And soon after that it all began to fall apart.

The liberal catholics kept building on the popularity and success of ASB. A hugely popular private publication, *The Cloud of Witnesses*, provided short biographies and readings for the ASB calendar of minor saints. *Lent, Holy Week and Easter* brought the renewed Roman Catholic liturgies for the season to the Church of England. The compilers of that volume were so pleased with the result that they repeated the effort with *The Promise of His Glory – From All Saints to Candlemas*, an entirely artificial liturgical season but offering some useful resources. The formality of preparing for *Common Worship* – the millennium replacement for ASB – refocused the liturgical work and produced some excellent new material for the eucharist: new eucharistic prayers – the great prayers of thanksgiving at the heart of the eucharist – and new seasonal material for use throughout the service, from the opening sentences to the final blessing. But even as the material became richer it was being used less and less.

The 1980s saw the spontaneous emergence of the Family Service. Promoted as a service for all the family, it offers an hour of children's entertainment in place of the Sunday liturgy. In evangelical churches liturgy had been almost deliberately dull – in the low-church style – since the reformation: Family Service looked fresh and exciting, and suddenly it was everywhere. As the fashion spread any attempt to include the legal minimum of ASB content was abandoned and every Family Service minister was making it up as he went along. It was the era of the charismatic-evangelical merger: the evangelical minister with the microphone was convinced he could impose the charismatic experience on his congregation if only he made it up as he went along, and made them smile and made them laugh and made them sing choruses, and told them what to do. Family Service became an unscripted one-man show fishing for applause, ultimately combining the tritest of liturgy with the harshest of evangelical fundamentalism. In 1989 the church authorities gave in to the inevitable and set a new lower minimum standard of items to include. Even this lower minimum has been universally ignored. Across the entire evangelical wing of the church they are making it up as they go along.

The millennium replacement for ASB could have been little more than a light revision: some of the language was beginning to sound dated and some features had stood the test of time better than others. Instead the Liturgical Commission aimed for a completely new book from cover to cover. *Common Worship* was rushed into print for the arbitrary millennium deadline, and was nowhere near to being ready. The new eucharistic prayers are unpolished, becoming confused about whether they are addressing God or the congregation. Some are so packed full of responses that everybody has to follow the book: intended to engage the children, they actually succeed in distracting everybody. The extensive seasonal material is of inconsistent and often poor quality. The collects – the prayers for each week of the year – represent a complete loss of nerve after the confident vernacular of ASB. They were designed as a return to the style of the Book of Common Prayer, using deliberately archaic language. In the second week of their national launch they called on every minister in the church to use the word 'succour' in public with a straight face. They were so bad they have already been replaced.

The baptism service suffered the same fate: universally condemned, it has been supplemented with alternatives that simply take us back to ASB. And nobody quite knows where *Common Worship* begins and ends. The main People's Edition bears little resemblance to the President's Edition. Both need to be supplemented with the latest drafts of initiation services, pastoral services, daily prayer, supplementary collects and a collection of Series One (1966) services reauthorised for occasional use. The ordination services are still in preparation. Nobody much cares because nobody feels committed to using any of it anyway: they stay with or go back to ASB, or they make it up as they go along, or they look elsewhere, to contemporary Roman Catholic material or the 1985 service book of the Anglican Church of Canada.

The Canadian book has sold steadily in the UK since publication on the basis of word-of-mouth recommendations, and was acknowledged after the *Common Worship* collects debacle as being in widespread unofficial use. The Liturgical Commission could have adapted the Canadian or Roman Catholic collects when their own first attempt was universally derided, but instead they set about composing an entirely new set themselves, with the inevitable consequence that the new set is not exactly the best available.

ASB 1980 created a decade of forward-looking unity in the Church of England. Its formal withdrawal from use in the year 2000 brought that era to an ungracious close. *Common Worship* was an unworthy replacement, first reviled and then ignored. Now every congregation is doing its own thing and the church is left with nothing to hold it together. On the day of its national launch *Common Worship* had sold so few copies that only one Church of England churchgoer in ten would have a copy in their hands. The Church of England has always been a church defined by its liturgy. That liturgy now defines it as a church with no half-decent resources of its own, a church where everybody makes it up as they go along, a church that in twenty years has gone from confidence and unity to ineptitude and division.

The Church of England's theological colleges encourage that division. Eleven remain at the time of writing, each an independent foundation, and each by heritage, history and culture a partisan foundation. The motto of the most drily and doggedly protestant – Oak Hill in north London – is 'Be Right and Persist'. We can look askance at their arrogance but it sets the tone for the whole network.

In the 1980s Oxford had three Church of England theological colleges, one for each party of the three-party church. Wycliffe Hall on the Banbury Road – between the academic centre of town and the comfortable north Oxford suburbs – was self-consciously protestant-evangelical. Saint Stephen's House – a mile out of town to the east amongst the terraced housing off the Cowley Road – was self-consciously anglo-catholic in the traditionalist mould. Ripon College Cuddesdon – seven miles from the centre in a one-pub one-shop village – did its best at being humble and magnanimous but knew that in contrast to its neighbours it was at the natural heart of the contemporary Church of England, being the merger of a catholic and a liberal college. Everyone we encountered as we moved through the system from first enquiry to training college was sympathetic to the liberal catholic consensus of the time. Even one-time evangelicals recognised the liberal catholic consensus as the true heart of the Church of England, and themselves as guests within it.

The ethos at Cuddesdon put the catholic into liberal catholic. We imagined that in our life beyond college we would share with our fellow clergy a strong sense of collegiality, common purpose, mutual support and community;

that there would be continuous learning, sharing of experience, a sense of interdependence and shared vision, built around the scriptures and the daily prayers of the church; that we would be a community united under the supportive local bishop, our shared 'father in God'.

While the culture and ethos were catholic, the teaching was not. There was no formal teaching of catholic practice or theology. Ecclesiology and liturgy were taught as history, not contemporary reality. We were taught how to be ruthlessly efficient managers – from keeping an effective filing system to getting our own way at a meeting – but we were never taught what it might mean to be a priest.

The teaching at Cuddesdon put the liberal into liberal catholic. In tutorials, seminars, essays and dissertations all credal affirmations were strictly optional, in the quest for a non-prejudiced liberal openness and inclusivity. The only near-compulsory credal affirmations were women's ordination and left-wing politics. Everything else was optional: the miracles, the resurrection, the uniqueness of Christ, the existence of God, the entire Bible. Being left to work it all out for ourselves was a great liberation, but the college declined to provide even a framework. The effective conclusion of the college's teaching programme was that Christianity could be whatever you wanted it to be.

This version of liberal theology asked all the right questions but offered no answers, which is like knocking everything down then offering no help to build it up again. The tragedy of the absence of any framework was that we were never formally taught the positive aspects of a liberal theology. Throughout the theological syllabus we knew all about what we did not believe and virtually nothing about what we did believe, perfectly fulfilling the negative stereotype of liberal theology, rejecting aspects of Christian tradition one by one until nothing remained. It offered little to enrich or sustain. Ultimately it could be as lifeless as its arch-enemy, fundamentalism. We were left to work out the positives amongst ourselves.

One of my fellow students drew great encouragement from the possibility that none of the biblical resurrection stories was literally true. If all that the first disciples had was a spiritual inner conviction that Jesus was alive as God for evermore, then our experience of the risen Christ is the same as theirs. We are on a par with them rather than missing out on the special privilege of the first resurrection appearances. The gospel accounts become poetic renderings of a profound shared experience: 'he was there with us in the garden'; 'he walked with us on the road'; 'he was right there with us in the room'; 'he restored my brokenness'; 'we recognised him in the breaking of bread'. Another observed that miracles prove nothing of value even if they do exist. If stage magician Paul Daniels came into the room and made a sturdy wooden table float in the air it would tell us nothing particularly useful about Paul Daniels or God or how to live our lives. Any meaning is in the context. Touch a leper for healing, and the context gives the meaning (a religious law declaring lepers unclean and therefore not to be touched). Heal a Samaritan (racially and culturally despised) or a woman with a haemorrhage (also declared ceremonially unclean) or the servant of a Roman centurion (representing the despised occupying powers) and the context gives the meaning. Dine with tax collectors (collaborators with the Roman enemy) and prostitutes and other notorious sinners, and the context gives the meaning, and that one is not even a miracle.

We looked down on the evangelicals who – instead of using the liturgy on Sunday morning – would make it up as they went along. But when the liberals talk about God they do just the same: they make it up as they go along. Far too many believe nothing with confidence at all. The contrast with fundamentalist leaders – who can hold forth in detail on every imaginable subject with absolute confidence – could not be more extreme.

The one exception to this lack of positive liberal teaching was in biblical studies. We all arrived at college having given up on the fundamentalists' doctrine of biblical infallibility, but had little more to replace it than the slightly embarrassed sense that while some of the Bible is helpful and wholesome much of it is not. Biblical studies at Cuddesdon was a wonderful new beginning. We learned how to read the Old and New Testaments not primarily as sacred scripture but as literature first of all, with all assumptions stripped away: we were reading a nation's collected folklore, or its highly edited official history, or accounts of the same events told from different perspectives for different reasons, or a complex fable offered as a contribution to philosophical debate, or a book of poetry, or hagiography, or letters from a feisty apostle to highly complex communities in awkward pastoral situations, or careful accounts of the gospel from different perspectives for different specific readerships. The bible came alive again. We felt betrayed as we discovered that this liberal biblical scholarship had been advancing for a hundred years, but four generations of clergy had been embarrassed by the opposition it provoked amongst a handful of evangelicals and so had kept this important scholarship to themselves. It was a classic failure of courage and conviction by the liberals that did not bode well for the future.

In 1991 we were ordained into the final decade of the three-party church that had existed since the first Elizabethan era, interrupted only by the English Civil War. It had survived relatively peacefully for more than three hundred years and we saw no reason to believe that it would not continue indefinitely, except of course that in the ongoing evolution of ideas the liberal catholic truth would continue to increase its subtle influence on liberal, catholic and evangelical parties alike.

Of course it was not to be – and the tragedy of the present fundamentalist domination of the Church of England is that it was made possible by the liberals' greatest triumph. The great unforeseen consequence of the ordination of women to the priesthood in 1994 was a devastating shift in the centuries-old catholic-protestant balance in the Church of England.

The ordination of women was primarily a liberal and liberal catholic agenda. Evangelicals hardly believe in the concept of ordination anyway: they drifted indifferently towards the acceptance of women vicars alongside women police constables, women doctors and equality of opportunity more generally. The catholic wing of the church does believe in the concept of ordination – essential to the good ordering of the church – and was split right down the middle: liberal catholics dogmatically in favour, traditionalist catholics dogmatically against.

Looking back now, it becomes clear just how far

separated the liberals and the traditionalist anglo-catholics had become. They had emerged as natural partners from the catholic and liberal revivals of the nineteenth and early twentieth centuries, and instinctively supported each other right up to this point. But the Church of England's liberals had taken the modernising spirit of the Second Vatican Council (1962–65) on board and were running with it, now treating the General Synod (established 1970) as an ongoing Third Vatican Council for their own rolling agenda of reforms, while the traditionalists had spent thirty years doggedly ignoring the modernising reforms of Vatican II: they were, and they are, stuck in an anglo-catholic time warp somewhere between the 1890s and the 1950s.

Numerous concessions were added to the legislation in the final months, weeks and even days before the vote, in a desperate liberal attempt to drive the measure through. More concessions were added in the weeks and months following, for the sake of the supposed unity of the church. In the end opponents had the right either to leave with a hefty pay-off, or to stay in a newly created quasi-independent church-within-a-church. The General Synod and the House of Bishops hoped their carefully worded concessions would be gently used, and would dissolve into irrelevance over a number of years. Instead the arrangements became hardened and formalised. Presented with a wide range of options, parishes settled at the two extremes, either accepting the full logic of the new mixed-gender priesthood or opting out entirely into the separate church within a church, where the all-male priesthood is preserved for ever 'without compromise'.

The concessions known as Resolutions A and B allowed a

parish to decline the services of female clergy by varying degrees. Resolution C created the church-within-a-church, allowing a parish to reject its bishop for the crime of endorsing the ministry of women priests elsewhere, and choose its own bishop instead: the Provincial Episcopal Visitor or 'flying bishop', untainted by any association with women priests. Theoretically the flying bishops serving the Resolution C parishes operate under the authority of the diocesan bishops, with Resolution C itself merely petitioning the diocesan bishop to set up the arrangement. No diocesan bishop was ever going to refuse, but neither synod nor bishops had realised where it would lead. For all practical purposes the Resolution C parishes have opted out of the life of the Church of England and their local diocese altogether, and formed themselves into a new national network. This network has its own bishops – the official concession made in 1993 – and has also acquired its own theological colleges, magazines, newspapers, weekly pew sheets, clergy chapter meetings, lay gatherings and national events, all the paraphernalia of a cohesive and well-functioning denomination. Previously lost and ill-defined within the broad mainstream of the Church of England, the traditionalist anglo-catholic network now has a clear sense of unity, purpose and identity. Far from withering away or dissolving into irrelevance it is thriving with a new-found self-confidence.

Within months of the first ordinations of women in 1994 the traditionalist half of the catholic wing had all but left the Church of England, with a consequence the liberals had not foreseen: a devastating, epoch-changing shift in the centuries-old catholic-protestant balance inside the Church of

England. The protestant-evangelical wing was used to a good push and shove with the equal and opposite force of the anglo-catholic wing, the habit of centuries. Still naturally ebullient, it discovered – to its great surprise – that its most strident opponents had left the building. Only a handful of liberals remained, tender-hearted and committed to compromise. Now, whenever the evangelicals pushed, the liberals would move. A new era had begun, in which the ordination of women itself was the least significant change of all.

During their years in the ascendant the liberals had effectively hung a banner over the church saying 'All are welcome here.' It was the liberal celebration of the old establishment assertion that you are a member on account of being a citizen unless you actively opt out. 'All are welcome here' is a liberal article of faith, affirming the inherent goodness of all people. It determines the liberal attitude to women in the priesthood, and towards homosexuality. Tragically, from ASB onwards, it also determines the liberal attitude towards the intransigent and the intolerant.

The ASB era was the great era of unity, but the first seeds of the current distress are hidden away in the very pages of the book itself. A tiny minority of protestant absolutists had refused to countenance using the service around which the rest of the church would soon unite – the new modern-language order for holy communion – on account of its Roman Catholic origins. The numbers involved would not register a single digit on a scale of percentages – the church was genuinely uniting around its new book – but the liberal establishment was concerned to maintain unity and did not wish to cause offence. They could have taken the trouble to argue the case, but to avoid the discomfort they made a concession instead: the intransigents were given their own small corner of ASB where the rest of the church would never go and which they would never leave. In 1980 a dozen pages in ASB created the first semi-official church-within-a-church, defined by its own formally sanctioned liturgy: a separate holy communion service in modern language but following the order, text and theological imagery of the 1662 Book of Common Prayer.

It was the first opt-out, the first concession to intransigence 'for the sake of unity'. The instinctively inclusive liberals felt generous and magnanimous – one small group had been kept on board rather than rejected – but they had unintentionally signalled that even intolerant and exclusive divergence was now welcome within the diversity of the Church of England. A welcome had been granted to intransigence for the sake of 'unity in diversity' – but intransigence itself has no interest in 'unity in diversity'. Once inside the building intransigence has its own agenda: to recruit, claim resources and condemn the rest. Those few pages in ASB set the precedent that would now destroy the Church of England.

Liberal and intransigent met again ten years later over the ordination of women to the priesthood. Liberals made concessions 'for the sake of unity', while anglo-catholic intransigence made ever greater demands. The bizarre result sees central church funding for an entirely new network, the membership requirement for which is a formal renunciation of the mainstream ministry of the Church of England.

The opt-out arrangements around the ordination of women could not have set the precedent more clearly. Any and every party, no matter how far out of sympathy with the mainstream Church of England, was now invited to move in, recruit, claim resources and condemn the rest. The fundamentalist elements within evangelicalism had previously kept a low profile for fear of the church's powerful liberal leadership, but with the three-party church reduced to a straightforward battle between liberal and evangelical, they now emerged to assert their natural role as leaders of all evangelicalism. They lead an evangelical wing reinvigorated by its merger with the charismatic movement and its uncensored abandonment of official Church of England liturgy. They can depend on the bland and predictable evangelicalism of the bishops appointed during George Carey's ten years as Archbishop of Canterbury. And in the era of global mass communications they are part of a network that is globally organised and phenomenally wealthy. Wresting control of the Church of England from the liberals is now a major focus of global fundamentalism. Wealthy Texan baptists loiter outside meetings of bishops to brief and debrief their fundamentalist colleagues inside. The liberals imagine a friendly parochial Church of England with a distinctive heritage of openness to all. Their opponents are global asset strippers interested only in driving out the enemy and taking vacant possession of the property and the structures.

The liberals have spent an entire century working as reconcilers, and being faintly embarrassed about the revival in their own scholarship and theology. Even in their own training colleges they have come to define themselves entirely negatively – by what they do not believe rather than what they believe – perfectly fulfilling the fundamentalists' caricature and establishing no framework on which to build a case on any subject. Most significantly and most tragically, this century of liberal self-denial 'for the sake of unity' has included a public abandonment of liberal biblical scholarship. Failing to engage with the scriptures intelligently themselves, the liberals have handed the entire biblical agenda to the fundamentalists, abandoning their own greatest asset and handing it to their opponents to use as they will.

The liberal church is in deep denial about what is happening. Liberal optimism still dares to believe that setting an example of tolerance will produce tolerance in others, that setting an example of generosity will produce generosity in others, that setting an example of gentleness will produce gentleness in others, and that the pendulum will swing in their direction once again. They have not reckoned with global fundamentalism and its God of wrath and condemnation. The liberals should be fighting back but they do not know how. They do not understand fundamentalism and they do not know how to fight. Unable to muster their own proactive agenda their response is always reactive, handing the fundamentalists the power to define the terms of the entire debate. The liberals are left sounding as though they have nothing positive to contribute and no convictions of their own. The confrontation will proceed in only one direction unless what is left of the liberal church can find its own voice to challenge fundamentalism head-on and even condemn it, and find the confidence to match the fundamentalists' level of conviction and commitment.

PART III

The Theme That Will Not Go Away

CHAPTER 7

The Insider's Story

The conflict between liberal and fundamentalist needed one practical issue to bring everything into clear focus, one specific issue where incompatible theologies would lead with absolute clarity to incompatible outcomes. Homosexuality became exactly the right topic at exactly the right time. It directly affects only a classically despised and hidden minority, and it brings theoretical issues into a clear practical focus.

The terms of the current debate on homosexuality had been set as early as 1983. I already knew the party line from countless evangelical sermons, articles, books and magazines, which delighted to discuss the topic in pornographic detail. To a teenager in 1983 the prejudices of the time were part of the natural order of the universe, a wholesome natural instinct to reject the bad and affirm the good. The party line simply matched those prejudices but turned up the volume for impact. To understand the battles in the church today we need to revisit that time, and the bizarrely diverse experiences of being gay in the church in the decades since then.

A couple of days into the week at the fifth Spring Harvest in 1983, I transferred from the main adult events to the youth programme. I had just turned sixteen. Much of the youth programme was led by Heartbeat, a Christian pop group and youth ministry combined. One morning halfway through the week they were doing healings live on stage. They would call out specific needs in the room made known to them by 'word of knowledge' and people with those specific needs would go forward to the stage for prayer. Some went up on stage to declare that the moment the need had been mentioned they had been healed. One teenager was up at the microphone demonstrating the bending and straightening of his arm after having had a bad elbow all year.

Evening healings, growing in number and bravado as the week progressed, were deferred from the meeting itself to the counselling room – the adjoining hall – after the meeting closed. Long lists of categories of people were invited: those who wanted to give their lives to Jesus, those who wanted to receive the holy spirit, those who needed help or healing. The team would offer general invitations – 'if you need to repent of something significant in your lifestyle' or 'if you have been drifting away from God and want to give your life to God anew' – and those based on supposed 'words of knowledge': 'God is showing me someone with a heart condition and God wants to touch your life tonight,' or 'God is showing me someone who has had an abortion and now has medical complications,' or 'God is showing me three people in here tonight who need healing in their relationship with their parents.'

All of this was received with a background murmur of supportive prayers as the music continued. The atmosphere broke only once. 'God is showing me four people' – a pause – 'four people who are struggling with homosexual feelings.' The speaker had not finished, but the atmosphere was broken: there was a cackle of laughter from several places around the room. Perhaps a handful of fringe teenagers had been struggling to take the evening seriously and the sombre mention of homosexual feelings pushed them over the edge. Those on stage recovered the situation, carrying on as if nothing had happened. 'If that is you tonight, God longs to heal you tonight. Join us for prayer in the counselling room after the meeting, and God will set you free tonight.'

Four is a laughable number. The proportion of gay young adults amongst evangelical and charismatic young people in 1983 was almost certainly higher than in the general population. It was not macho or cool to be Christian but it provided a superb network of supportive friends who talked endlessly about love for God and one another and hugged whenever they met. For the closeted and self-loathing misfit that was the gay teenager of the early 1980s it provided a community of rescue, safety, security and intimacy. The sub-culture's hatred of the homosexual's misdirected emotions only mirrored the homosexual's own. There were more likely to be forty gay teenagers in that room than four.

However many were in the room, only one responded to the call. Across the floor of the packed counselling room after the meeting teenage seekers and adult counsellors paired off for counselling, prayer and direction, sitting or kneeling in their asymmetrical pairs. I guess most were seeking ministry that was routine and well-practised: recommitments, prayers for the holy spirit, confession and absolution. When the one gay teenager who had responded told his adult counsellor why he was there the counsellor seemed shocked and out of his depth, and went for reinforcements. That teenager knelt alone in silence contemplating the healing that finally lay ahead, having been called by God to this perfect moment of grace. Slowly the room emptied around him. Half an hour passed. Finally with only two or three other teenagers remaining in the room a whole team of adults gathered around that sixteen-year-old, headed by the nationally known figure who was leading the youth programme that week. By the time this was over only that teenager and that team would be left in the room.

I knew all the supposed reasons why healing sometimes did not happen: the person praying did not have enough faith, the person prayed for did not have enough faith, the person prayed for did not really want to be healed, or the prayer was not in line with God's will. That night I knew that every box was ticked for this healing to take place. I wanted it more than anything else in the world. To show willing I had already had one serious Christian girlfriend. I was surrounded by a top team of nationally known charismatic leaders, I had been called by word of knowledge and I had responded in absolute faith.

With the formality of a court of law I was asked only to confirm my name and the reason for my being there, and then the prayers began. In many ways it was a beautiful moment. I was kneeling with my eyes closed, sitting on my ankles with my head down by my knees. Around me a mixed group of adults knelt and 'laid on hands', touching their palms against a shoulder or upper back. Each in turn was offering prayers for my life, my welfare and my walk of faith, giving thanks for the years that had brought me to this place and praying for the future.

Finally it was time for the main business of the evening and for the leader of the group – the leader of the week – to take charge. He prayed for all of us as we prepared for the moment of grace into which we were all to be drawn, a moment of freedom, healing and wonder. As his prayers moved towards that moment he gave thanks for all of God's great works in the world, until finally the moment came and he began to pray for the healing. The others offered 'Amen' and 'Yes, Lord' ad lib.

And then I had a role. I was invited to say: 'I renounce that spirit of homosexuality.' The team waited, holding its collective breath. I spoke the words. They all prayed out loud together, 'rejoicing' and 'claiming the victory'. I headed back late to the accommodation walking on air, convinced that a new chapter had begun.

I went straight from Spring Harvest to a conference for teenage ordinands (candidates for ordination) in Oxford, organised by the national Church of England vocations board. It was full of wonderful young people committed to faith and life with a whole variety of diverse experience on the pilgrimage of faith. There was a daily shared life of prayer in the chapel and food in the hall. There were talks, seminars, discussions and workshops. Liberal bishops sat with us on the floor as we worked through ideas and talked about the life of faith. A large group of us talked all night on the last night and watched the sun rise over the dreaming spires.

By the middle of the week it was evident that something was awry. I kept on falling in love with all those wonderful teenage ordinands, and not in a way that Spring Harvest or I could approve.

Saint Paul was my comfort that summer. In the second letter to Corinth he writes: 'To keep me from becoming conceited at the abundance of revelations I had received, there was given me a thorn in the flesh, a messenger of Satan to torment me. Three times I pleaded with the Lord to take it away, but he said to me: My grace is sufficient for you, and my power is made perfect in your weakness.'

It was a mysterious and costly gift, this thorn in the flesh, but by that autumn I had begun to acknowledge the more positive aspects of stereotype: that it might become a gift of gentleness and creativity, of understanding, caring and generosity. Perhaps the celibate priesthood called, characterised by a greater availability and a deeper commitment to the role. It emerged that the tougher inner-city parishes were cared for almost exclusively by bachelor priests – assumed to be discreetly homosexual – as the married priests fled with their families to the comfortable suburbs. That suited my idealism. My home parish even had a positive role model: a stylish thirty-something bachelor, popular with everyone and with a discerning spirituality, working in the caring professions and living alone in the loft apartment of a warehouse he had bought and converted for himself and for his parents who lived on the floors below, and where guests were always genuinely welcome. I nurtured a self-image for the future as a celibate bachelor priest, bearing this costly grace.

By August 1985 I was just weeks away from leaving

small-town Lancashire for the undergraduate years. For ten days I went on retreat, travelling round the Scottish Highlands on my own, camping and youth-hostelling, driving an old Morris Mini that I had bought with £200 of my own gap-year earnings. I sat on bare rock miles from anywhere looking out to sea and marvelled at the beauty of creation. Love seemed close and all-important: love and humility, a humble openness to the heart of another. Perhaps that way lay intimacy. I knew intimacy in many Christian friendships, and its physical expression in a touch and a handshake and a warm embrace. It made no sense that intimacy between a man and a woman could continue indefinitely, while the path towards the intimacy that I desired was closed. It was not even clear exactly where the prohibition lay. Could you live together? Share a room? Share a shower? Most of all it made no sense that any such law should be so arbitrary. If God was a God of compassion there had to be a reason. I justified the biblical injunction by persuading myself that some of those imagined acts could never be honest expressions of love. The mystery was precisely which. I resolved that if I focused on humility and love I would recognise the limits of their expression as they approached, and need not fret or feel shame in the mean time. I knew I could not yet say it, but I formed the words in my mind: 'I am a gay Christian.' I still knew of no one else who had thought these things through before.

I headed for Europe with a one-month rail pass and a Christian friend from school, still a significant adventure in the days before budget flights and in the era of the Berlin Wall. Someone pointed us towards an English-language bookshop in Paris where English-speaking backpackers could sleep upstairs in exchange for a couple of hours' work in the shop. An American and another Brit invited us to dinner in the Latin Quarter. We enjoyed a pleasant evening and split the bill. They offered to meet up again at midnight to show us some of the nightlife. At their regular nightclub as we descended from street level it became clear – as we had suspected – that this stylish, colourful music venue attracted young adults almost exclusively male. It felt like a home-coming: these were my people. Everyone danced the night away. In the cool Paris air later we each turned down the invitation to go home with one of our hosts. Two weeks later we spent a week in the village of Taizé joining in the silence and the simple music of the daily prayers with the brothers of the Taizé monastery and hundreds of other young people from around the world. I knelt in silence and offered to God whatever lay ahead.

I was only briefly back in my home town before leaving at last for the undergraduate years. I was glad to be leaving behind so much history – and my still-conservative evangelical church – to begin a new part of the journey: three years reading philosophy and psychology at Jesus College, Oxford. My swansong was at the harvest supper, preceded each year by a mixture of contributions humorous or holy. I stood alone with my guitar and sang poignant songs of human longing for the divine. They applauded rapturously. Some were in tears. I left the next day.

I learned that year that there are many honest expressions of love. I fell in love for the first time, no longer fearing the emotion. Halfway through the second term there was a Valentine's-night party. I spent the evening trying to charm him. The next day I asked him out. He smiled sadly as he explained: he had spent the evening trying to charm a mutual friend, and apparently she had spent the evening trying to charm me. He bought me flowers and a card and wrote out a poem and signed it 'with love'. I kissed the back of his hand. We all stayed friends. I was walking on air.

I fell in love again. I remember the first embrace as perfect beyond all imagining. It felt as though we were melting together and could never be apart. Falling asleep and waking up together were so beautiful. For the sake of biblical infallibility I clung to the idea that certain physical intimacies could never be honest expressions of love. By the end of the year I had let the idea go. Four terms in – in the final days of the calendar year 1986 – I sat in my student apartment mid-vacation overlooking the garden and wept for the loss of my religion. Through my teens I had clung to a faith that declared the bible consistent and infallible in Old Testament and New. I could cling to it no more. I was back where my journey of faith had begun before I ever met the charismatics and evangelicals who filled my teenage years. I was back with a God of infinite compassion who looks on every human being as a beloved child of God, and with Jesus, his limitless compassion and his sorrow so profound.

The relationship ended in tears and I spent a year forlorn. Then I broke all the rules by falling in love with one of the friends who was helping me through it. We got together as our finals ended, and we are together eighteen years on.

I finally attended a Church of England selection conference in summer 1997, two years into undergraduate life. That autumn I was presented with a bewildering choice of potential theological training colleges. I discussed the options with my undergraduate college chaplain, an evangelical by heritage. He warned me that three of the colleges were 'basically homosexual' and that I might be shocked. He named the three.

I knew I was no longer an evangelical. The only other label I knew was anglo-catholic. I decided to visit the most famous and highly regarded of the anglo-catholic colleges, at Mirfield in West Yorkshire, run by a community of monks and held in high esteem. It was one of the three the chaplain had named. I had no idea what to expect.

The atmosphere at Mirfield was relaxed and informal, even though the students wore their cassocks for much of the day. The college's sense of community was built around a common life of prayer in the chapel and meals in the refectory. Beyond that, student life was much as I knew student life already, except that it was almost exclusively male, which I now found more unbalanced than I expected. On the final evening of my visit almost the entire student body moved to the nearest pub for the evening. They drank beer, ate free servings of cold cuts, and talked loudly and raucously about each other's mighty pythons and lances. It was not what I expected, and it was not what I was looking for. There were three main anglo-catholic colleges and the pattern was much the same at each. A colleague who went for interview at one of the other two had one of the host students standing outside his guest room at around midnight, coughing politely, expecting an invitation in.

Back in Oxford, I could have returned to the prospectuses to carry on the search but two members of the chapel choir resolved the matter. They were training for ordination at Ripon College Cuddesdon. After weeks of speculative discussion they finally picked me up by the elbows and took me off to see the college. Not many weeks later I was there for interview and ready to stay. The atmosphere was relaxed and informal. There was a sense of community and belonging. There was ASB liturgy in church and chapel and there were shared meals in hall. There was a balance of male and female students and a whole range of ages. At four o'clock the garden doors swung open and tea and cake were served on the terrace in the sunshine overlooking the valleys and hills of Oxfordshire. Students, staff and spouses chatted in groups. Children of the married students ran by playing games in the grounds. I thought: 'This'll do.'

At Cuddesdon, homosexuality was discreetly affirmed as a subset of a strident anti-sexism. Anti-sexism and the ordination of women were at the top of Cuddesdon's agenda in theology, liturgy and general culture. Given the culture of the wider church nobody would say anything in public or to any tutor about their own sexuality, but there were no secrets within the student body, and most tutors let it be known that, whilst discretion remained the best policy within a conservative church and society, all sensible theological opinion was moving in the same direction. About a quarter of the college was gay.

Early in our middle year the 1989 Osborne Report was completed. A panel of experts – appointed and commissioned by the House of Bishops – concluded that it was time to recognise permanent, faithful, stable homosexual relationships within the church. The bishops decided the report was far too radical for the laity in the parishes or the evangelical wing to bear, and sought to suppress it. Its authors were so annoyed that there was hardly any point wondering which of them had leaked it to the press: they all had. It was widely published but never formally acknowledged by the church. For those of us in college the report was an affirming vision of a future we believed was just around the corner.

The official 1991 report, *Issues in Human Sexuality*, contained just enough to allow gay clergy to remain in post with some degree of integrity. The report asserted that in so far as the Bible mentioned homosexuality at all it was generally negative, and that this was reflected in the tradition of the church, but so many respected theologians were now taking a different view that the church could no longer cast out homosexual couples and instead must welcome them. It then asserted that this liberty could not be claimed by the clergy for themselves because they have to epitomise a higher standard – a morally confused argument that also introduces a moral separation of clergy and laity unprecedented in four hundred years of Church of England history. Despite this conclusion the bishops would not become 'more rigorous in searching out and exposing' gay clergy. On the contrary, the clergy would be welcome to share their homes with their long-term same-sex companions and it would be improper for anyone to assume anything irregular in such an arrangement or to 'infringe their right to privacy' by questioning them on the subject. The policy was 'Don't ask, don't tell.'

I now know that this key section was written not by the report's authors but by the House of Bishops, with each party fighting over its key words and phrases in a desperate attempt to find a text they could all sign.

Despite the report there were intermittent campaigns throughout the 1990s by obsessive fundamentalists determined to be more rigorous in searching out and exposing gay clergy even if the bishops would not. Most of the campaigns were run by just two individuals, David Holloway of Jesmond and Tony Higton of Hawkwell in Essex. With society at large still mostly hostile to the idea of gay clergy, and the church hierarchy at best ambivalent, most gay clergy chose to keep their heads down and get on with being clergy. In the entire decade only two Church of England parish priests came out as gay. The confidential database of the Lesbian and Gay Christian Movement lists more than eight hundred self-identified gay clergy who have had contact with the movement, many of them in long-term stable partnerships. I lived quietly in my little curate's house with 'my friend from undergraduate days', and kept to the 'Don't tell' policy. Before I moved to my second curate's post I made sure I had the support of my new vicar. I realised after a year there that I knew the people and the place well enough to survive any unwanted exposé. I would keep my head down for a few days while it all blew over, then maintain a dignified silence and get back to work.

Not many months later I found myself staring into the abyss that could have meant putting that plan into action. We had a major event planned in the parish, a turf-turning ceremony for the construction of the new church and community centre. As well as being the curate responsible for the new church I was chair of the Community Association that had secured the funding and would now build, own and operate the centre on behalf of both church and community. With less than twenty-four hours to go, I had a phone call from the local independent radio station. I responded cheerfully, expecting to be asked about the event planned for the next day, but that was not the reason for the call. 'A clergyman in Essex has declared in his parish magazine that all gay clergy and those who support them should declare themselves and resign. How do you respond to that?'

There was silence for a while as the words hung in the air. They spoke first. 'Is now not a good time? Shall we call back in a couple of hours?' They were handing me a stay of execution.

I called the archdeacon for advice. He was not surprised and said I should refer the radio station to the diocesan press office, and might like to speak to the press office myself for reassurance. I called them and they knew immediately what was going on. 'Tony Higton again. We spend all our time clearing up his mess. Just refer them to me.'

I calmed myself and waited. When the radio station called back it was to apologise. They had been put up to it. They had been told that I was some kind of gay rights spokesman and had been encouraged several months before to make my presence in the town into a news story. The trendy young adults who ran Harlow independent radio decided that 'There is a gay man in Harlow' did not count as news, so Mr Higton wrote his piece in his parish magazine and called back saying 'now it's news'. Reluctantly they called to see if there was half a story. As soon as they realised I was not the national spokesperson that I had been made out to be they were appalled that they had been used, and appalled at the thought that they had caused someone an afternoon of anxiety. They could hardly have been more apologetic. They turned up sheepishly with a tape recorder the next day to cover the other story.

You forget that homosexuality is an issue when it is just your ordinary life. I forgot as I applied for the post of warden of the diocesan retreat house, a twenty-three-bedroom house set in delightful gardens in a small Essex village with a programme of residential and day events throughout the year. It needed somebody with both a breadth of spirituality and a talent for organising major projects. With ecumenical experience in Harlow and having chaired the new building project there – by then with dozens of staff and an annual turnover well into six figures – everything seemed to fit.

They had advertised twice and failed to appoint. I had not been looking for a move, but heard about the vacancy at deanery chapter in January 2001, and was encouraged by the assistant rural dean to apply. I made a tentative phone call to the diocesan office asking to see the paperwork. The next morning the phone rang at 8.30 a.m. and it was the bishop. I had not yet seen the papers and he virtually offered me the post. Within forty-eight hours he had assembled the entire interview panel of twenty-two on a weekday for a full day of interviews. It turned out that the chair of the interview panel was my former archdeacon, a supporter of gay clergy who knew my situation. I was appointed unanimously.

A few days later I met with the bishop for a first discussion about future plans: more accessible literature, flexible programmes, new programme ideas aimed at a wider constituency, closer integration with parish and diocese, open house and open garden programmes, and simple alterations to the layout of the building which at the time was arranged entirely in single rooms with no facilities.

By convention clergy appointments are kept under wraps until a formal announcement is made simultaneously in every parish affected. We agreed to make the announcement the Sunday after I returned from holiday, six weeks after the interview date, on the first Sunday of Lent. I would leave the parish six weeks later on Easter Day. In the mean time all the arrangements began. The welcome service in the new parish was planned, complete with all the diocesan dignitaries – a nightmare of diary coordination. Assistant bishops, archdeacons and training officers phoned to say how pleased they were with the appointment and how much they looked forward to working on the various plans. There was a diocesan synod meeting where everybody seemed to know already and sidled up with quiet congratulations. It was the talk of the diocese.

I spent the final week before the announcement date working out how to tell the Church Langley congregation. I planned the service around the idea that the church is a community of people, not a building or a hierarchy or any particular priest. On Saturday as usual I made the final selection of hymns for Sunday and printed the weekly bulletins, then settled in the upstairs sitting room to relax for what remained of the evening.

At 9.30 p.m. the bishop rang. I was delighted at this sign of his ongoing interest and encouragement. He asked how I was, and I told him some of what I had planned for the morning. The bishop then explained the reason for his call. He had had an anonymous phone call making allegations about my home life, and he wanted certain assurances. This was not what I expected six weeks after the appointment and less than twelve hours before the announcement.

An awkward conversation followed lasting almost an hour. It was ten years since *Issues in Human Sexuality* had come out and ten years since I had read it. I could not remember a single phrase of the relevant section but I knew the general argument. I was open with the bishop, as *Issues* invited me to be, about living with my long-term companion, and I declined to say more, as *Issues* not only advised but insisted. It was not enough. The bishop needed further assurances. I assured him that in ten years of ordained ministry I had said nothing in public or in private contrary to the teaching of the church as set out in *Issues*, and had no intention of changing that policy. It was still not enough. He could not bring himself to talk explicitly about sex but it was perfectly clear what he wanted to know, as no other assurance would do. He was breaking the rules, asking questions he was not supposed to ask.

It was thoroughly unpleasant, but about 10.15 p.m. that first phone call came to an end. I had persuaded the bishop that the announcement should go ahead. At 10.25 p.m. the bishop called again. He had thought it through and now he wanted the announcement delayed while he considered the issues in more detail. We argued. I had spent all week preparing the service. I had already told key people in the parish. The announcement juggernaut was in motion and could not be stopped without casualties. The bishop conceded that a provisional announcement could be made, a break with etiquette but saving face. Overnight I remembered that the announcement was going ahead in a whole range of partner churches. It was simply not possible to contact them all reliably before the start of their Sunday morning services. If every other church in the area was announcing the appointment it made no sense to make a different announcement at my own church, and in any case a provisional announcement would make the bishop look foolish and indecisive. The appointment would surely go ahead because *Issues* was perfectly clear on the matter. For ten years I had faithfully kept to my side of the deal, and the appointment had been unanimous. The bishop just needed time to realise that the policy served to protect everyone involved, himself included. He would take advice from his wise archdeacons and assistant bishops. He would have resolved the matter within forty-eight hours and I could save him any embarrassment by pretending those late-night rule-breaking phone calls never happened.

There was no point trying to sleep. I called an acquaintance of many years, a senior priest I had known since before ordination who had been a colleague in one diocese and then another. He was furious at the turn of events and I ended up slightly embarrassed and trying to calm him down. Dozing by 11.30 p.m., I was woken by the phone. It was my priest friend calling back. I picked up the receiver and he just began. 'How dare they! How dare they! And who is looking after your pastoral care right now? Who cares about you? How dare they! An anonymous phone call? Who the hell acts on an anonymous phone call? How dare they!', and so on. I was cheered but even more embarrassed. I needed sleep and I had a difficult service ahead.

The announcement went according to plan. There were good wishes and hugs all round. People asked my partner whether he was looking forward to the move. We had not really known until that day that they knew such an assumption to be appropriate. It was very affirming for us both.

There were tears in my eyes during the preparation of the altar – I had chosen one of my favourite classic hymns – and again at the breaking of bread. The congregation thought they were tears for saying goodbye to this church. For the preceding hours I had stayed focused on the task of making the announcement. Having completed that task, I was suddenly overcome by the seriousness of what had happened the night before. As I stood there at the altar those tears were for the possibility that I was now saying goodbye to my entire priesthood.

For the next ten days the focus was on convincing the bishop. I was called in to see him at the diocesan office and interrogated again. By then I had checked the text of *Issues* and was able to quote it point by point. He was clearly in the wrong. All he had to do was put the appointment back on track, and if challenged refer to the document and his 'thorough investigation of the matter' in line with the terms of the document. He did not commit himself either way. I think he genuinely had not decided.

Nearly a week passed. He called me from his mobile and left a message asking to see me that evening. I picked up the message late in the day. I was due to be leading the latest part of our parish programme called Through the Bible in a Year, a smart home-grown multimedia presentation across thirty Tuesday evenings. I chose Bible study over a meeting with the bishop. It went well. I saw the bishop the next day. 'Michael, we have some hard talking to do.' There was no talking to do at all: a sacking can be achieved in a phone call or a fax. 'I hope this doesn't affect our future relationship,' he said. I was overcome by an unfamiliar calm as I replied. 'A priest in a diocese this size would only expect to have dealings with the bishop if discussing a move, and I do not expect that I shall ever be considered for a move within this diocese while you are still its bishop.' The bishop looked away. 'I suppose that's right.' I stared out of the window. I resented the tear in my eye.

I had my full response prepared. 'I'm going to take a sabbatical. I'm going to leave on Easter Day as planned and come back later in the year.' The bishop objected. 'Well, if you look in the diocesan guide you will see that you can apply to the relevant department for a sabbatical.' I interrupted, overcome once again by that unfamiliar calm: 'You are a bishop, and you make and take appointments. I am an incumbent with the freehold and I am taking a sabbatical. Clergy have been to prison and come out again and still had the freehold. I am taking a sabbatical.' The bishop conceded: 'Perhaps it would be a good idea.'

That Sunday, as a church, we should have been counting down the last four weeks until I left. Instead I began the service by saying that I was staying. They cheered. 'Their loss is our gain!' shouted one. There was applause and the mood was bright. It became like a celebration. I made up something about 'unforeseen tensions emerging at the retreat house in the wake of the appointment'. Afterwards they were cheerful with me, but they were taking my partner to one side, gathering round and embracing him saying, 'You must be so upset.' They knew.

I promised them I would come back later in the year. That promise may well have been the only thing that did bring me back. The four weeks up to Easter were a blur.

Holy Week was powerful. Easter Day was a wonderful celebration. They presented me with my leaving present – a watercolour of the new church, presumably commissioned when they thought I was leaving. There were mixed emotions all round. Many thought I would never come back.

For the first two months of the sabbatical I was moved to tears at every service I attended. That was part of the mix of emotions. Another was fury at the injustice of a church where a bishop could behave like this with impunity, and at the refusal of anybody in the diocese to challenge him. Before the next meeting of the retreat-house trustees each one of them was phoned individually and told that the incident was not to be mentioned. The meeting proceeded as if the entire sequence of events had never taken place. Even in my own deanery chapter those who would be privately supportive sat in silence as the fundamentalist vicar of the neighbouring parish launched a scathing attack on my integrity. Just one said, 'I'll talk to you afterwards.' I had spent all those years taking such care, in public and in private, never to say anything that could be quoted against me, as *Issues* demanded: a huge personal sacrifice for the sake of the unity of the church. Now that sacrifice had been spat back in my face. And the way the bishop saw me now was so pathetically obsessive. Two weeks before when he looked at me he saw a whole human being made in the image of God, full of faith in Christ, youthful energy, a breadth of spirituality and the financial and presentational nous to turn around the ailing retreat house. Now all he saw were 'genital acts'. That is a strange and rather disgusting obsession. And there was another twist of the knife: a gay priest in a partnership had only months previously been appointed to a senior post in the diocese by that same bishop. Did that priest lie to give the assurances demanded, or was there simply no malicious phone call prompting the questions to be asked? It is a strange way to run a multi-million-pound organisation, or a church.

I looked out of the hotel window over midtown Manhattan and contemplated the options. I could expose the hypocrisy of the bishop, in synod and beyond. I could sue him under employment law and become a test case in the European courts. With the help of some retired campaigning lay people I set part of the process in motion. Three thousand miles away a formal question was put at diocesan synod: did the bishop support the policy laid out in *Issues in Human Sexuality*? He said that he did, but we all knew otherwise.

I continued researching the options but eventually backed away. I could define myself as a victim in the international courts and the media spotlight, or return to my ordinary priesthood and my ordinary life. After four and a half months I returned to the parish and we had the best three years ever. We built up the lay leadership team and wrote ourselves a constitution. We celebrated the faith in music and liturgy and word and sacrament. We mourned two of our own members, burying one in the pouring rain. We baptised an adult member who added to her testimony a spontaneous dance. We married two of our members in the middle of a Sunday-morning service, and gathered every Sunday, Tuesday and Thursday to read the scriptures and break the bread. They were the richest years in ministry by far. I had chosen this role from many options, the congregation was delighted that I had come back, and I knew I had the support of every assistant bishop and archdeacon in the diocese: when I returned from sabbatical in late 2001 they were falling over each other to offer me team rectorships and senior incumbencies. I chose to draw a veil over the chaos of the year, and to live my ordinary priesthood to the full in the place that I knew.

Halfway through those three confident years I had a bizarre encounter with the fundamentalist minister of a local independent church. He had left a message asking if he could see me. I was suspicious, as I had never had cause to have any dealings with him, but I thought it best to play it by the book. I arranged to meet him in the chapel of the church and community centre, a safe space, well over-looked. When we met he explained straight away that he had heard something 'shocking' about my home life – 'that you have moved in to live with your homosexual lover' – and he wanted the facts. The phrase amused me for its inaccuracy. Clearly salacious gossip is best expressed in the most emotive form available. I was also amused that the 'shocking' allegation was such old news: we had been in Harlow for nearly ten years. I calmly explained that there was no secret about who lived in the extensive vicarage of the parish. It was occupied by myself and an old friend from undergraduate days who worked in the area. He was an active lay member of the church – regularly elected to various posts within the church – but he was a parishioner and I had no intention of discussing his private life or mine any further than that. After the business with the bishop and the retreat house I was not going to be fazed by one local independent minister.

I do not know what he was expecting, but the calm

response fired up his anger. 'Will you deny it?' he demanded. I would not discuss it. 'Then you will not deny it!' he declared with triumph. 'You may keep your silence but I know in my heart what you are doing!' He explained loudly that it was now his duty to rebuke me, which he set about doing at some length. I began to observe the situation in a rather detached manner. A self-appointed independent minister I had never met, with no training and no oversight, was presuming to rebuke, on the basis of his own imaginings, a properly selected, trained and ordained minister who had the support of colleagues, archdeacons and bishops – barring one diocesan – within the ancient and established church. I was not answerable to this man, indeed it was his self-righteous and judgemental invasion that was reprehensible. I interrupted him and explained the alternative perspective: that in many people's view the hatred he promoted was responsible for millions of ruined lives down the centuries, that it had led to murders and persecutions and had kept millions from knowing the love of God, and that even today one child in every GCSE class has contemplated suicide because of the hatred that he represented. For all of this, he and his like were responsible. He was on his feet. 'How dare you! How dare you!' he hollered. 'You are refusing to repent! I must now do my duty and raise this matter with the other ministers in the town! God will remove you! God will remove you!' And he fled.

The next day I had a call from Walk Through the Bible Ministries. In the course of the conversation in the chapel I had explained my commitment to the serious study of the scriptures, and mentioned my work as a Walk Through instructor as evidence of that commitment. Walk Through the Bible is a seminar series that gives an overview of the entire Old Testament in just six hours. When it came to our town it was appreciated equally by people who had only just joined the church and by people who had been reading the Bible daily for forty years. I learned more about what is actually in the Old Testament in six hours of Walk Through than I did in three years at theological college, where we had learned how to analyse an individual text but never had an overview of the Old Testament as a whole. I was so impressed that I trained as a tutor. Liberal friends wondered why I was involved with 'a bunch of Bible bashers', and I wondered why they thought teaching people what was actually in the Bible was somehow a bad thing, when it empowers people to counter the biased, arbitrary and often straightforwardly false claims of the fundamentalists.

The director of Walk Through was gracious and calm when we met, but unless I could give him the assurances he now needed, my time with Walk Through was over. I argued that in the discipline of my church the questions he was asking were neither to be asked nor to be answered. It was not enough for him. Unless I could give him the assurances I required I was no longer suitable for work in their ministry. I was to return all the teaching materials as soon as possible. I delivered them to the project office on a day when I knew he was away, as there was nothing more to say.

In the mean time a rambling two-page handwritten letter arrived from the fundamentalist minister of the chapel encounter. Gleeful at my dismissal from Walk Through – only the beginning of what he had planned – it went on to give various detailed instructions about public statements I was now to make and actions I was to take, and set out what he would do if his orders were not fulfilled, including calling a town conference of ministers and going to the press. I had no intention of taking any notice of his instructions, and I was unconcerned by these two specific threats, but on reading and re-reading the letter I realised that it probably constituted an attempt at blackmail, could be the first stage of worse to come, and therefore ought to be filed away as potential future evidence, should it be required. I could not bear the thought of having something so repulsive in the house so I surrendered it into the care of the rural dean.

For advice on what might happen next I called a retired gay priest in the area, a one-time campaigner. He laughed out loud as I recounted the story, especially that it had taken the minister ten years to catch up with me: 'He's had a go at every bachelor priest that ever passed through the town.' He assured me that nothing ever came of it and I should forget the whole episode.

I had another appointment out of town on the day I met the director of Walk Through for my dismissal. I went straight from the one meeting to the next, which was with the bishop who had 'un-appointed' me for refusing to answer the same questions two years previously. A handwritten postcard had arrived suggesting that he would be happy to meet again, if I wished, before his impending retirement. I was intrigued.

It took him half a dozen attempts to spit it out, but he wanted to apologise. He regretted all that had happened and the inevitable hurt it had caused. 'I see the spirit of Christ in you, Michael, I really do. I always have done.' We talked about my ministry and his retirement plans. I drove home feeling strengthened, reassured, justified, and even healed of a wound.

The intervention of such moments is part of the complexity of a war within a church. For decades this man in his late sixties has used one particular set of assumptions to make sense of his experience of God. In his head he is fearful that pulling this one thread will unravel the entire fabric of the faith of those years. His heart sees other things: it protests and disagrees. The casting vote lies with his gut reactions. In 2001 his gut reaction was not to proceed with an appointment. In 2003 it was to mend broken relationships before he retired.

We met again in 2005, at my initiative. I now had a story to tell, and I wanted to be gracious in the telling, as he had been gracious two years previously. I put to him the head–heart–gut explanation. He said that it was a helpful insight, but there had been no further development in his thinking on the subject. There was little more to say. We talked about the future of the church, our respective local churches, our homes and gardens, our current work, responses to the tsunami. It was a meeting of Christian people no longer constrained by office. A disagreement remained, and was best not mentioned again. I suppose I must remain to him a perplexing anomaly, a paradox that cannot be resolved.

I bear no malice. It was a long time ago. It feels like it happened to somebody else. But it did happen, and the story deserves to be told. It should be known that even with gentle and gracious bishops the result of an unacceptable theology of homophobia is potentially devastating for individual lives. Every week for thirty years the office of the

Lesbian and Gay Christian Movement has received calls telling stories like my own. The general secretary pleads with the callers to tell the world what is happening inside the church, but weighing it all up they have preferred to carry on with their damaged lives in privacy.

CHAPTER 8

Jeffrey John and the Aftermath

My own experience in 2001 reflected the growing confidence of the evangelical fundamentalist wing of the church. When George Carey announced his retirement as Archbishop of Canterbury late in 2001 the fundamentalists were convinced that the post was theirs to claim, as virtually every other post had been under his leadership. When it became clear that the liberal Archbishop of Wales, Dr Rowan Williams, was a likely appointment, they did all they could to prevent it, with exaggerated threats and unprecedented public campaigning. In summer 2003 they were still smarting from the failure of that campaign, their first significant setback in a decade of creeping advance. All the resentment and bitterness surrounding that failure was poured into the new campaign against Jeffrey John.

Like thousands before him, Jeffrey John had been deliberately discreet about his homosexuality throughout his ministry. His qualifications and background meant that a post as a minor bishop was long overdue. In summer 2003 he was appointed to the post of Bishop of Reading by the

Bishop of Oxford. The appointment was endorsed by Rowan Williams in his role as Archbishop of Canterbury, and announced as a matter of routine by Buckingham Palace. A few formal complaints from the fringes on the day of the announcement had been anticipated, but the sustained and growing campaign that followed had not. Weeks after the announcement, the campaign against the appointment was still growing day by day, dominating the mainstream national news and showing no sign of losing its momentum. Eventually Rowan acted: he called Jeffrey John down to Lambeth Palace and made him write a letter of resignation to Buckingham Palace.

I heard the news of this final indignity that afternoon from an editor at the *Guardian*. Two weeks earlier as the storm had been brewing they had commissioned a piece – published anonymously – on life as a gay vicar. I emphasised its overwhelming ordinariness, interrupted from time to time by sudden intrusions of unprovoked hatred from complete strangers who were invariably fundamentalist ministers of one kind or another. They gave the piece a page to itself. When they heard that Jeffrey John had spent most of Sunday at Lambeth Palace being made to resign they called me for a response. They tried to feed me the lines: 'Are you angry?' Actually I was glad for Jeffrey John's sake that it was all over, and submitted five hundred words to that effect. 'What a relief it is that Jeffery John has resigned. He would have spent the next twenty years being pursued every day by curtain-twitching snoopers, being looked at askance by everyone he met, and achieving nothing of any real value. Nobody needs to waste their time and energy like that – especially someone of the calibre of Jeffrey John.'

I lamented the final demise of the Church of England as the archbishop gave in to the arbitrary demands of a co-ordinated fundamentalist campaign. I sent it off before the end of the afternoon but heard nothing back.

Bizarrely, I had an appointment to see Rowan Williams at Lambeth Palace the next day. I had known Rowan during my undergraduate years in Oxford, and after my sabbatical in 2001 I wrote to him to see whether he might look at some work I had done on the enneagram (a tool for spiritual development) and perhaps write a commendation or even introduce a publisher. He agreed, but while the manuscript was in the post George Carey announced his retirement as Archbishop of Canterbury and Rowan's life became rather complex. In 2003 I wrote again and the meeting was rescheduled for a Monday afternoon several months ahead; the day before the meeting, the Jeffrey John crisis broke.

I fully expected a call cancelling the meeting, but it never came, so at lunchtime I set off for Lambeth Palace. I bought a newspaper on the way. The article I had submitted was across the bottom of the front page. I found the right gate in the palace wall and spoke to the gatekeeper. I was directed through the grounds towards a great stone staircase. At the top I was ushered along a corridor and into the state drawing room. The room had once been grand but was now rather tawdry, which felt like an analogy for the Church of England as a whole. The chandeliers were plastic, with crumpled tin foil covering the screws and bare wires at the tops of their supporting chains. Bare metal brackets protruded from the wall, supporting the mirror above the fireplace, the wallpaper torn, the holes not filled, exposed in their original rust-proofing red. The chairs and sofas were tired and none of them matched. The fireplace had been boxed in cheaply with plywood, painted black with screws and laminated edges exposed. Strange objects – like random gift-shop items – sat on mismatched antique cabinets.

At the appointed hour I was called back into the corridor. The staff spoke in hushed tones, averting their eyes. 'The archbishop went down that way, so if you wait here he should pass you on his way back.' Rowan invited me into his study then sat looking blankly into the distance. 'Not a great weekend then,' I ventured. 'No, not a good weekend.' Someone else brought in the tea but he served it himself. I suggested that I felt rather out of place in a palace and he said that he did too. Eventually he composed himself and the mood lifted. He asked me how I was and what had I been doing, and what about my book. He was warming to the opportunity to talk about anything other than the events of the previous afternoon. Soon he was sitting on the edge of his seat and we were both back in Oxford. I was the student with a thesis to present and he was the passionate tutor who knew every relevant text. Within minutes he was quoting the desert fathers in Greek and making connections with a whole range of disciplines. He said he would be happy to write a commendation, even a preface.

The conversation moved on from the future of the book to the future more generally. I suggested the church was divided in so many different ways there was no point pretending any longer that there was one united church. He nodded sadly in agreement, and asked, 'But what do you do?' I suggested that the model is already out there, and the model is the resented but thriving Resolution C network. I

suggested that every parish should join a new network: resolutions D and E, F, G, H, J and K. There could be an Alpha
churches network, a liberal catholic network, a civic
churches network. They could each have their own ethos
and policies and structures. We should leave them to thrive
or fail on their own merits. He was nodding throughout, as
if to indicate that he had already considered this model in
detail as a viable solution. I pointed out that there was
nowhere in the model for forty-three regional offices, which
he acknowledged with a shrug, and that ultimately there
was no place for an umbrella body called the Church of
England: even this caused no more than a raised eyebrow.
When I suggested that the Church of England might continue as a land-management agency he seemed entirely
content.

'And if there's no place for a Church of England there is
certainly no place for an Anglican Communion.' The
Anglican Communion is the worldwide network of thirty-
eight separate national churches around the world with
historic links to the Church of England. 'That figure of seventy million members they keep quoting includes thirty-five
million English people who never see the inside of a church,
and half the rest are in Nigeria. If it really is so important to
them all they'll manage perfectly well without England.'

Now I had lost him. He was going to defend the Anglican
Communion. It was an important global non-governmental
organisation. Africa had been treated badly: we owed them
a major role in the Communion as some kind of payback
for the harm we had done to them. I let it pass. I still needed
that preface.

We talked some more about the various parties in the

church and their differences. Then he asked what I thought about the situation now for gay people in the church. What could I possibly say, after his sacking of the publicly celibate Jeffrey John the day before? So I laughed it off: 'It doesn't bother me. I'm out of here in eleven months.' He was totally focused again. He looked shocked and numb. He actually went white. 'What?' – as if he had misheard. I was embarrassed at the response I had provoked. 'I'm leaving,' I explained, apologetically: 'What is there to stay for?' Feeling exposed, I summoned my defence: 'I'm actually behind the game on this one. Half my college contemporaries have already left.' It took the focus off me but only made it worse for the archbishop. He had no idea things were so bad. But we were out of time. He was still in shock as we shook hands goodbye. On the way home I wondered whether he would read all the newspaper coverage of the day before, and recognise in an article by an unnamed gay priest some of the phrases from our conversation, and make the connection.

In January 2004 I announced to the parish that I would be leaving that summer. I was under two book contracts and I had some television work. There were new directions to explore. They were sad for themselves but full of good wishes for all that lay ahead.

A few days later I received a rambling piece of hate mail from the fundamentalist minister of the chapel encounter. He was gleeful and triumphant at my impending departure and looking forward to my replacement by someone who would 'teach the truth about sodomy and sodomites'. The pointless, venomous hatred was shocking after the good will and best wishes of the parish. I was taken aback. I should have been able to shake it off, but I could not stop thinking about this pathetic man, who knew nothing about my life, crowing in triumph, full of hatred, and boasting of that hatred to the people around him as a proud mark of his religion. Several of my deanery colleagues considered him an ecumenical partner and worked with him regularly on various projects. I read and re-read the letter, seeking any justifying factor: a question or proposal or suggestion. There was nothing. Its sole purpose was the exultant expression of hatred.

I couldn't settle back to work. I clicked around the web for definitions of hate crimes and how they were handled. The Metropolitan Police encouraged victims to report every incident. Homophobic abuse had a section all of its own. Harassment and hatred were defined as anything perceived by the victim as harassment and hatred. I found the equivalent page for Essex Police, a rather less strident affair warmly introducing the smiling staff member responsible. I called the local station to ask what might happen if I decided to report an incident. Only minutes later, I had been allocated a crime number and promised a visit within hours from two investigating officers. I felt human again. The oppression of irrational hatred had been broken by a hearty affirmation from the machinery of the modern British state.

As I waited for the officers to arrive I wondered what I was doing. I considered the biblical mandate on how to deal with those who do wrong or cause distress within the Christian community. It assumes structures of leadership and oversight. An independent minister has no oversight apart from the law of the land and the police, so by involving the police I was following the biblical mandate in the only manner available. Later I read that the act of turning the other cheek requires the assailant to hit the victim like an equal, not like a slave. Translated to the modern era the injunction to turn the other cheek is not to continue in the role of a hidden victim but to run into the street shouting, 'Come out here and hit me again, where everyone can see you for what you are.' By involving the police I was inviting him to repeat his hateful attack where everyone could see him for the worm that he is, swirling around in the cesspit of his own hatred.

I also reflected on the extent to which society had changed in only a matter of years. The notorious Section 28, slipped into the Local Government Act of 1988, was vaguely phrased and never tested in a court of law, but had both the intention and the effect of preventing virtually all discussion of homosexuality in schools, even in sex education. It played shamelessly to the popular prejudice of its time. As recently as 1999, Conservative leader William Hague sacked frontbencher Shaun Woodward for supporting New Labour's attempt to repeal Section 28. The repeal only made it through the House of Lords in 2003. Now in 2004 the police were actively pursuing a minor independent clergyman for making statements no more shocking than those made over Section 28 in the Houses of Parliament the year before, and by the end of 2005 gay people would have the civic dignity of partnership legislation virtually identical to civil marriage. In 2006 the social acceptance of same-sex partnerships feels like a timeless part of tolerant English culture, but in reality it is a very recent phenomenon: a post-1997, post-Diana, New Labour phenomenon.

When the officers arrived they were supportive and sympathetic, even shocked at the tone of the letter. It was all the evidence they required: a crime had been committed. One even expressed it in theology: that God could not possibly be on the side of such a repulsive man. 'Isn't it all about loving one another?'

It was agreed that I would recover the blackmail letter from the year before. It took ten days for the rural dean to admit that he could not find it, during which time a second piece of hate mail arrived, as crowing and pointless as the first. The police took both and confronted the man. He argued for an hour about his religious rights but they were unimpressed: a hate crime had been committed and no religion could justify that. He finally agreed to accept a caution rather than face prosecution. He is now a minister with a criminal record – for a hate crime.

I am glad to say that there was growing unease in the town at the high profile of the new independent churches. The situation was confused considerably by the involvement of three Church of England parishes in their network, called Together for the Kingdom, and the absence of any alternative ecumenical council of churches for the town. From the three Church of England parishes already involved there was heavy pressure on the others to recognise Together for the Kingdom as the representative body for all the churches in the town, but it was a bizarre organisation. In preparation for their millennium project they reissued the open invitation to all ministers in the town to join them. When I attended their next meeting it soon became clear that I was the only person to have taken up the invitation. I was simply ignored as they argued over the minutes of their last meeting, then reopened the business of that meeting in an attempt to overturn its decisions. Eventually they moved on to plans for their millennium project. After some minutes I raised my hand and introduced myself and some of what I might have to offer. I then endured several minutes of abuse, the general thrust of which was that I clearly had no interest in praying for the town or working with others as I had not joined the group until now. Two other ministers arriving new to the town – one the year before and one the year following – had the same experience of sitting in the room while the others discussed whether or not they should be allowed to stay. All the other parishes in the town were wise enough to stay well away. A few carefully phrased questions later revealed that the parishes never joined anyway: this was a gathering of ministers who sat in judgement on each other as individuals, not an association of churches. One of the three Church of England ministers pulled out, but they kept the name of his parish on their notepaper for kudos. The Methodist and United Reformed Church ministers kept well away. The Roman Catholics were very clearly unwelcome anyway.

By 2004 there was growing unease across the town at the high profile of Together for the Kingdom. A liberal Church of England parish and a Roman Catholic priest together called a meeting to discuss setting up an alternative town-wide network. Thirty ministers attended, including one of the Church of England ministers associated with Together for the Kingdom. Everybody stared at their feet as he gave a long address, attempting to recruit people into their latest project 'because we all agree on the basics'. One brave Catholic priest argued at some length that we do not all agree on the basics at all. Everybody else stared at their feet. I missed the next meeting as I was dealing with the police over the hate-crime incident. At a third meeting, the last before I left the town, numbers were down below a dozen. The meeting was again dominated by a Together for the Kingdom recruitment campaign, this time by the new rural dean. The few remaining liberals stared at their feet and wondered what to do. I started to argue the original case for an entirely separate network; the rural dean argued against it. I countered by telling them how bad it could become, with the police becoming involved as one minister in the town sent venomous hate mail to another. The liberals all stared at their feet. 'Oh, him,' said the rural dean, smiling: 'he's just a bit of a maverick.'

CHAPTER 9

Use and Abuse of the Bible

The great mystery of the twentieth-century liberal catholic era is not just that it was so gay-friendly – with gentle-spirited liberal catholics in charge, that was virtually inevitable – but that it was so heavily gay-populated as well. On reflection it does make sense. For the life-long bachelor the ordained ministry of the church used to offer a life with structure and purpose. It offered a network of collegiality, mutual support and even intimacy, in the parish and in the priesthood. According to the classic catholic model, the demands of the priestly role are in any case incompatible with marriage: priests are invited to be married to the church instead. And as the opposite has so often been said, let us seriously consider the possibility that gay people actually make better priests: they have a more objective outsider's perspective on mainstream society; free from the demands of childcare and a modern marriage they have more to give to the life of the church; they have generally had to think more seriously than most about some fundamental life choices; and they have usually experienced suffering and rejection before finding in their faith a sense of redemption, a valuable path for any priest to have walked.

In the vocations departments and selection procedures of each diocese of the Church of England in that era there was no interest in enquiring about the sexual orientation of ordinands: there was a simple and open welcome based on faith and experience, and a sense of vocation. With the high population of gay clergy it made no sense to ask. At my own selection conference they were concerned only to ensure that I did not have any interest in imminent marriage, as such a thing would impact significantly on the cost of any residential training programme.

For the entire twentieth century until its last decade the bounds of tolerance were the same: it was fine to be gay but it was best not to tell the laity; indeed it was best not to say anything on the subject in public at all. That was the internal consensus of the church at all levels. As an idealist in my early twenties I was appalled to discover this hypocrisy: a church maintaining one consensus in public and another in private. I had suffered years of distress as a teenager and had been abandoned to travel my pilgrimage alone while the majority liberal church hierarchy looked after itself and said nothing in public for fear it should 'upset the laity'. Thankfully others perceived the same dissonance and from the 1970s onwards a whole series of church reports – some published, others suppressed – recommended change. The compromise of *Issues* in 1991 was accepted by the liberals, at no small personal cost, 'for the sake of unity'. At least the debate was finally out of the colleges and into the public domain.

The arguments over homosexuality have been rehearsed repeatedly in society as well as in the church over the last forty years. Now the argument in society is over and in the church only two issues remain. The first is that gay sex is somehow dirty and unhealthy and repulsive to all decent people. This argument appeals to an ever smaller constituency; most people recognise that imagining your heterosexual friends having sex is not exactly enriching and beautiful either, and some things are better neither discussed nor imagined in too much detail.

The second issue is that 'The Bible is against it.' Here at least there is room for some serious debate. For anybody who takes the scriptures seriously, the Bible is not unambiguously 'against it' at all. Stable, faithful homosexual relationships as lived out in a contemporary liberal democracy are not discussed in the Bible at all, any more than party politics, air travel, hip replacements or contraception. And the few references that supposedly do set the Bible against homosexuality are a rough collection: in the entire text there are just two verses in Leviticus, and two words and one paragraph in Saint Paul.

The two words in Saint Paul appear in long lists of sinners, alongside murderers, kidnappers, perjurers, idol worshippers, adulterers, thieves, drunks, revellers, robbers, the greedy and the deceitful. One of the two words – *malakos* – means 'soft', and is used elsewhere in the New Testament to describe fine clothing. The other word – *arsenokoites* – is unknown in contemporary Greek literature, although it is used in later Greek literature to describe an undefined act which can apparently be either heterosexual or homosexual. The use of the word 'homosexual' as a translation for either *malakos* or *arsenokoites* reflects only the prejudices of the translators and their editors. Similarly, the use of the word 'sodomite' for 'male temple prostitute' in most American translations of the Old Testament is entirely gratuitous. The damage done by these idle slanders is immeasurable. (The word '*malakos*' appears in 1 Corinthians 6:9, '*arsenokoites*' in the same verse and in 1 Timothy 1:10.)

There is just one paragraph in the New Testament that makes unambiguous reference to homosexuality, in Romans chapter 1. This sees Paul shocked to find – in the context of a wider sexual depravity – that some men lust after other men and some women lust after other women. This previously unknown state of affairs he blames on idolatry – the worship of created things instead of the creator – which Paul also blames for envy, murder, strife, deceit, gossip, slander, insolence, haughtiness, boasting, disobedience of parents, faithlessness, heartlessness and foolishness. The offence is an objectifying 'idolatrous' lust, and the context is a more general sexual depravity. It is similar to the observation of Jesus in the gospels that 'a man who looks on a woman with lust has already committed adultery with her in his heart': the sin is the sexual objectification of another – not presumably heterosexuality *per se*.

Those two words and that one paragraph are all the New Testament offers on the subject. The rest is in the Old Testament, from before the time of Jesus. The book of Leviticus – an Old Testament holiness code – declares that a man 'shall not lie with a male as with a woman'. Amongst many other things the holiness code also bans the trimming of the beard and the weaving together of two different twines, as in a polycotton shirt. Somehow these rules do not awaken the same zeal in most evangelicals. The Old Testament law also gives detailed instructions on the buying and selling of slaves, including a special section on selling your own daughter as a slave. It also commands genocide, forbids marriage to foreigners, celebrates polygamy and bans the lending of money at interest. Clearly the evangelical claim to be following the Bible is somewhat arbitrary in its application.

We should visit Sodom briefly. The culpable sins of the city of Sodom are defined in Ezekiel chapter 16: the people were arrogant and overfed and did not help the poor and needy. Elsewhere they are described as proud and haughty and inhospitable to travellers. Several of these crimes come together in the scene in Genesis where every adult male in the city joins a mob that appears to intend violence upon two visitors described alternately as 'angels' and 'men'. Surrounding the house where the guests are staying, the mob shouts, 'Bring them out that we may know them.' The biblical 'know' has a sexual connotation only one time in a hundred. Such a connotation need not be assumed in this initial scene of general mob violence. The sexual horror of the event is introduced by Lot, who is hosting and protecting the angels, when he attempts to appease the mob by offering them his two virgin daughters for the night, presumably for a gang rape. This story is supposed to illustrate Lot's righteousness in contrast to the evil of the other city dwellers.

Less often quoted is the almost identical story set in the city of Gibeah. This time the visitors are a Levite and his concubine. Once again the men of the city surround the house, demanding, 'Bring out the man that we may know him.' The unnamed host offers the mob one virgin daughter and the concubine. On this occasion the concubine is actually surrendered to the mob for the night and dies as a result of the ordeal. The Levite later tells the people of Israel that the people of Gibeah intended to kill him – nothing else – and that they raped and killed his concubine. This provokes a war in which seven hundred men from Gibeah join just twenty-six thousand from the surrounding country to face four hundred thousand warriors of Israel. They kill forty thousand of the warriors of Israel before the tide of the battle turns in Israel's favour. This story – almost identical to the story of Sodom – is less often quoted in the anti-homosexual cause.

The New Testament uses Sodom as an example of inhospitality and apocalypse. In only one place (Jude 7) is Sodom accused specifically of 'sexual immorality and perversion', a phrase with which translators have taken many liberties and readers have taken more. The original Greek text uses the word for fornication (*ekporneuo*) and then the phrase 'going after other flesh' (*aperchomai opiso heteros sarx*). The New Testament epistles follow a convention of Greek philosophy in using the world 'flesh' or '*sarx*' as shorthand for all morally corrupt human motivations and behaviours. 'Other flesh' ('*heteros sarx*') would be more authentically translated as 'other bad things' or 'other wickedness'. This renders the complete phrase most accurately as 'fornication and other wickedness'. The Greek word for 'other' is '*heteros*', as in 'heterosexual'. Sodom is accused of 'fornication and going after *heteros* flesh'.

And there we exhaust the Bible's entire commentary on the matter. The rest is special pleading – that there is a heterosexual assumption in places like the garden of Eden or in Jesus's discussions of human relationships – but the vast majority of the Old Testament also has a polygamous assumption, and 'the biblical model of marriage', a phrase much trumpeted by contemporary evangelicals, assumes not only polygamy but also concubinage, a good trade in marriageable daughters, and going to the marriage bed the same day a man meets a woman he intends to take as a wife. This is the true biblical model of marriage, and it is not what most evangelicals have in mind. Their use of the phrase is wantonly dishonest.

There has been a tit-for-tat response that answers one arbitrary reading of scripture with another, including a pro-homosexual reading of any close same-sex relationship. David and Jonathan have the shortest odds by far, but in the end none of this leads anywhere. The reality is that the Bible has nothing direct to say about modern homosexuality, any more than it has anything direct to say about speed cameras, the European constitution, pop music or the national curriculum. The real energy driving fundamentalist zeal on the issue is coming from elsewhere: from the insistence – in pornographic detail if necessary – that gay sex is somehow dirty, unhealthy and repulsive. This argument comes not from faith or scripture but from prejudice and a wanton lack of knowledge. Using this argument in the twenty-first century has the same credibility as maintaining that the earth is flat. It is the choice and argument of a cult. Fundamentalism leads and mainstream evangelicalism follows.

The energy for pursuing this issue is maintained amongst the fundamentalist leadership by the fear and discomfort that can surround all sexuality issues, especially for those who are uncomfortable with their own sexuality. Sexuality is a powerful experience not easily confined within the tidy boundaries required by an evangelical trying to earn his own salvation. There is also the fear implicit in departing from 'the timeless teaching of the church', by which is meant the prejudice of their own childhood, and the fear of departing from 'the in-crowd', their brotherhood and their only security for salvation. There is the fear of receiving upon themselves the hatred they have hitherto cast upon others, and ultimately the fear of their wrathful and condemning God. There is the self-righteous false security of being able to point at others and say, 'We are better than them,' and finally the strange titillation they experience as they discuss other people's sexuality – and especially homosexuality – in intrusive, pornographic detail.

Once 'the will of God' has been defined, anything can be called as witness. The lies told in the service of the evangelical campaign are hideous and shameful: bigotry dressed up as science, false anecdotes and assertions presented as proofs. Perhaps the worst lie of all is the repeated commitment to 'listen to the experience of homosexual people'. The fundamentalists and the current House of Bishops alike condemn first, and so cannot possibly listen or hear.

The fundamentalists will lose the argument that sex is dirty with all decent people in time, but the abuse of scripture deserves to be confronted head-on, and an alternative vision of the will of God presented positively and confidently rather than apologetically. Far from condemning gay people, the scriptures actually plead their cause against their detractors. The New Testament letter to the Hebrews says:

'In speaking of a new covenant God treats the first as obsolete, and what is becoming obsolete and growing old is ready to vanish away' (Hebrews 8:13): which is to say that the old covenant – the Old Testament law – has no role in the Christian era. Saint Paul is equally clear in Romans: 'We are discharged from the law, so that we serve not under the old written code, but in the new life of the Spirit' (Romans 7:6).

In Saint John chapter 16 Jesus himself says: 'I have many things still to say to you, but you cannot bear them now: when the Spirit of truth comes, he will guide you into all truth.' That guidance began in the New Testament era with the admission of the gentiles to the Christian faith without their first converting to Hebrew ways. The vigorous debate between Peter and Paul on the issue is recorded twice in the New Testament, sombrely in Acts chapter 15 and rather more feistily in Galatians chapter 2. In the same spirit many centuries later, as just one example amongst many, slavery was finally recognised as an unambiguous offence to Christian values, even though neither Old Testament nor New Testament challenges it at all. And just as the spirit of the gospels was pointing from the beginning towards the inclusion of the gentiles and liberation for the enslaved, so also it was pointing from the beginning towards the celebration of love in diverse and life-enriching ways for people of good faith. Like the inclusion of the gentiles and the abolition of slavery it was perhaps too much to bear at the time: 'I have many things still to say to you, but you cannot bear them now: when the Spirit of truth comes, he will guide you into all truth.'

And finally the words of Jesus from the Sermon on the Mount, presenting the heart of his teaching: 'Judge not that you be not judged, for the measure you give will be the measure you receive' (Matthew 7:1–2). In words and actions Jesus repeatedly condemns the patronising, self-righteous judgementalism of the religious leaders of the day, and invites everyone to join instead the complex liberation of the law of universal love.

In contemporary evangelicalism, the question of homosexuality has become the instant single-question test of theological 'orthodoxy', as though an individual's attitude to this one issue can tell you all you need to know about an individual's loyalty to 'evangelical truth'. It is indeed a very fine single-question test. To be negative about homosexuality is to be part of a cultic movement that places adherence to the cult itself higher than adherence to scripture, higher than rationality, higher than evidence or data or information, higher than the voice of the suffering, higher than compassion for the outsider or the neighbour or even for the self, and ultimately higher than truth.

A fashionable movement emerging from evangelicalism in the United States – with influences now in the UK – is called the Emerging Church network. It is a network where it is safe to have doubts about the divinity of Christ or the theology of the cross or the question of eternity. It is a safe place to question the nature of God or even the existence of God. All of this is happily discussed by its proponents, who are reducing everything to the essentials of Jesus in the gospels and a sense of community. But ask about homosexuality and you draw a silence followed by an awkward conservative response. The main UK proponent ensures that every book he writes contains at least one pitying anecdote about a sad homosexual, just to maintain his credentials and to ensure that his old friends know he is still onside. We have an emerging evangelical network where you do not need to believe in God or the divinity of Christ but you still have to be anti-gay. Finally we see where they stand.

The real tragedy in the current debate is the complete failure of integrity on the part of the liberals. On the single-question test of orthodoxy – 'What is your attitude towards homosexuality?' – their silence and ambivalence show more sympathy for the dangerous cult of contemporary fundamentalism than concern for the truth or for the good of the world and its people. The truth, and the dignity of homosexual people everywhere, have been sacrificed 'for the sake of unity' to the cult of fundamentalism. The latest sacrifice at the time of writing is the Anglican Communion, now officially a worldwide anti-homosexual organisation. It has carried out the first two expulsions in its history – the United States and Canada – for refusing to discriminate sufficiently against homosexuals. The churches of England, Scotland, Wales and Ireland stand with Nigeria and the rest as officially anti-homosexual institutions. This is not a price worth paying 'for the sake of unity': it is a betrayal of the very heart of the gospel.

There have been times when the church has been ahead of public opinion in doing what is right: in the struggle against apartheid, in the abolition of slavery, in the provision of healthcare and education for all. On the issue of homosexuality the church is so far behind public opinion – as well as being in the wrong – that it has become a very public disgrace to all that is decent, right and good. Perhaps both sides in the debate are unaware how much the world and the church have changed in the last ten years. In 2004 the entire European Commission was thrown out by the European Parliament because one member was on record as saying that homosexuality was a sin. I have moved back to the north of England with my partner and joined in the life of the village and of three Church of England parishes and nobody has even paused in welcoming us as we are, indeed we are actively sought out as interested newcomers for the many voluntary tasks of village and parish life. The world has moved on. The ordinary lay folks in the parishes have moved on, and they are betrayed by liberal and fundamentalist alike.

The debate should have been over the moment Rowan Williams' appointment to Canterbury was announced: the fundamentalists had done their worst to prevent it. Instead of dealing decisively with the issue, Rowan promised to put aside his own convictions and allow the majority view of the existing bishops to dictate national policy. The existing bishops had only secured their appointments by promising his predecessor that they would keep to the fundamentalist line on this specific issue: it was Rowan's previous refusal to make that promise that kept him out of England for so long (in Wales, where the church has been independent of the Church of England since 1920). Now he surrenders his authority to his predecessor's appointees. The fundamentalist grip on the church does not just continue, it is strengthened, as Rowan himself ends up defending and even advancing the fundamentalist cause 'for the sake of unity'.

Rowan allowed himself a moment of liberal lapse in supporting the appointment of Jeffrey John as Bishop of Reading in 2003. Any future hope represented by that appointment was over long before Jeffrey John was made to resign. It was over when it emerged that Jeffrey John had made a promise of celibacy, despite having been in a long-term relationship with another priest for twenty-seven years. Under pressure over the nature of the relationship, he confirmed that it was ongoing, a lifetime commitment and a gift from God, but that while it had been a sexually active relationship in the past, it had not been so for a number of years, and he accepted that this was the price of his continuing in ministry in the church. The price of tolerance for gay clergy rose that day from 'don't tell' to 'pledge celibacy,' or possibly 'tell a bare-faced lie.' When even that pledge proved insufficient for the appointment to go ahead it was all over for the liberal church.

A retired bishop recently reminded me that Jeffrey John would not have been the first gay man with a well-known partner to arrive at a meeting of English bishops. I was not pleased to be reminded of this long-standing hypocrisy. Outrage named ten practising gay bishops in 1999, and they were probably right on all ten counts. One currently serving bishop with a long-term gay partner claims in public never to have knowingly ordained a practising homosexual. All of them stand by the current policies of oppression and prohibition. 'How do they sleep at night?' I asked. 'I don't know,' he said: 'I don't know.'

The supposedly tolerant era of *Issues* finally drew to an ungracious close in 2004 with the publication of a new report, *Some Issues in Human Sexuality*. It contains a strong affirmation of the fundamentalist line and little more than a bleat from the liberals. We are left with an officially homophobic Church of England, an officially homophobic Anglican Communion, and a new method of appointing bishops even more bizarre than the old one: you now appoint according to the old system, and if enough self-appointed fundamentalist leaders complain loudly enough you withdraw the appointment and start again. There is now a sign over the door of the church saying 'Heterosexuals only'. No half-decent heterosexual would want to belong to such a warped and sickening organisation.

It is time for a serious progressive challenge – for the sake of the gospel – to the increasingly vacuous liberal establishment. This is not about being more liberal than the liberals: it is about having a faith and a theology with some substance, taking the scriptures seriously, having some concern for truth, putting right a hideous betrayal of the gospel, and maintaining gospel values without compromise. For a decent progressive theology there is an ideal single-question test of orthodoxy: 'What is your attitude towards homosexuality?' If you delay or fudge your answer you are betraying the heart of the gospel, at the cost of real human lives.

PART IV

The Future

CHAPTER 10

The Coming Financial Crisis

There is one final factor driving these times of change in the Church of England: a crisis in the finances of the church.

Just one generation ago the clergy were funded almost entirely by ancient endowments. The parishes would look after the parish church and the parsonage but the clergy themselves came free of charge. Some parishes – often the more ancient ones – had larger endowments than others. They were known as good livings, the living being the income of the benefice. Incumbents in those parishes could afford to employ curates, spend lavishly on the work of the church, enjoy a higher income and generally be held in high esteem within the church for having been appointed to such a fine benefice. In poorer livings clergy would work alone and struggle to make ends meet. For years there was no pension provision, but there was no compulsory retirement age either: clergy could hold on to their final benefice indefinitely, complete with house and income. Alternatively, if they made it into a good living, they could negotiate to surrender the benefice on condition that they receive a pension from its income thereafter.

In a great internal socialist redistribution in the 1960s all those parish endowments were gathered in and centralised at diocesan level. The clergy would all receive much the same stipend, and would be deployed not according to available funding but according to need, as assessed by the bishop and his team. There would also be a standard universal pension, and a compulsory retirement age. The new system resolved many financial anomalies, but also ended centuries of local autonomy, introducing instead a system of regional strategic planning. The parish was no longer an autonomous unit in a national network but a branch of the diocese with its centralised budget.

The new system had its supporters as long as the clergy still came to the parishes free of charge – as a gift from past generations – but with generous pension provisions and hearty salary increases over the last thirty years the historic funds have all but gone. All that remains is committed entirely to pensions, and to funding in perpetuity the posts of the forty-three diocesan bishops.

In the final decades of the twentieth century there was no point looking to parliament or the Crown for additional funds, so the church looked instead to the lay people in the pews. For centuries the only people with power in the church were monarchs, parliamentarians, bishops and clergy, in a top-down hierarchy. Now for the first time in history the hierarchy of the Church of England finds itself financially dependent on voluntary contributions from the ordinary churchgoing laity.

Diocesan quota had modest beginnings. It was gathered

in from the parishes each year to fund the diocesan office and small pieces of additional work like student chaplaincies. From the beginning the wealthier parishes would pay proportionally more: it was only fair, and it was never that much. It was met from the collection plate and other fund-raising activities.

The bishops began to realise just how much power the quota system represented. If they pushed the quota up a few points they could employ more central staff, under their own direct control and in their own offices: secretaries, personal chaplains, advisers and co-ordinators for everything from children's work to industrial policy, education and social responsibility officers, ecumenical and inter-faith-dialogue officers, international links co-ordinators, media officers, and development workers for everything from evangelism to liturgy. Over the last thirty years each diocesan bishop has disappeared behind a multitude of personal staff making it virtually impossible for the clergy or the people of the parishes to contact him and leaving him with no idea what is going on in the wider church beyond his own private entourage. This entire operation is funded by quota and controlled by the bishop, and has appeared from nowhere over the last thirty years. The Church of England has never been so top-heavy as it is today.

As clergy stipends rose, and the endowments were eaten away by inflation, overspending and pension provision, diocesan quota rose to fill the gap. At first it included a small contribution to the stipends fund. Now it is effectively the whole amount, with a contribution to future pensions on top. It is still managed directly by the diocese, and the wealthier parishes still pay more.

At deanery level the effect is starkly apparent. The smaller and middle-sized congregations continue to pay less in quota than their clergy actually cost, while the larger congregations pay for three or four clergy whilst receiving only one or two. In the local reality of deanery chapter everyone is struggling to bring in the money, and everybody knows who is subsidising whom. In an era of unity and affluence all might have been well, but bitter divisions in the national church combine with the financial crisis to set minister against minister in a battle both for their own parishes' resources and for the soul of the national church. It is here, in every deanery chapter nationwide – just as much as in Canterbury or General Synod or the House of Bishops – that the era of the united Church of England is drawing rapidly to a close.

As a rough guide, quota in most places works out at about £5 per church attendance: £5 a week for the regulars and £5 more each time anyone else wanders in. For a couple that means £10 a week, plus something extra to account for the visitors who only give coins. Half the congregation are pensioners so those of working age ought to give more. We are up to about £20 per week for a regularly attending couple of working age, just for quota. Local expenses, including all the costs associated with the building, will be about the same again. That makes the church budget dependent on a total contribution, from each regularly attending couple of working age, of about £40 a week, or £175 a month. It is fortunate that in practice the pensioners tend to give as much as those of working age.

In virtually every parish the quota is the largest single item in the budget by far. Each diocese continues to determine, supposedly on the basis of need, which parishes can have incumbents and which cannot, and which can have curates and which cannot. And each diocese tinkers endlessly with the formula for allocating quota: usually some combination of attendance figures, membership rolls, estimated salaries in the parish and actual parish income.

The status of quota was never enshrined in law. Legally it remains a voluntary contribution by the parishes to the diocese. Ten and twenty years ago if it came to an ultimatum the diocese could threaten to withdraw resources from a parish that refused to pay, although this would only become serious once the current vicar's security of tenure was removed by relocation or retirement. Now the diocese is so dependent on quota that the ultimatum works the other way around. Fewer than half a dozen of the largest churches in a diocese could bankrupt the diocese overnight if they jointly refused to pay. The increasing use of this threat by some large evangelical parishes is probably the most significant change in the local, regional and national politics of the Church of England in the last ten years. One of my college contemporaries observes that, if you can threaten to bankrupt your diocese, 'you don't need to win the argument'.

To the few who so far refuse to pay, add the many who simply cannot pay, as local funds are exhausted and the burden rises year by year. Quota collection rates are falling: 95 per cent, 90 per cent, 85 per cent. These are significant shortfalls counted in hundreds of thousands of pounds or more in every diocese. Forty of the forty-three dioceses are running annual deficits that will see them insolvent within a decade. Planned or unplanned, abrupt or phased, the present situation will come to an end. At the moment it looks like being unplanned and abrupt: the banks will refuse to process the payroll. The major comparable example to date is a cathedral now openly dishonouring its debts having had its overdraft frozen at £4 million, and the legal situation is unclear. Multiply it up and imagine, for this is what lies ahead for the whole Church of England.

I wondered for a while what would happen when the money finally ran out and there were nine thousand clergy to pay. I imagined weeks of stalemate between church and banks and government – this is the established church after all – concluding with a time-limited government rescue plan conditional on radical restructuring over a number of years. Then I realised it would be nothing so grand. The overdrawn cathedral settled out of court, paying each creditor some fraction of what was due. The professional organisers of a major event – who had worked for the cathedral in all good faith – were left heavily out of pocket. Chelmsford diocese balanced its books for several years by cancelling all maintenance and repair work on its clergy houses: a soft target. So when the bank freezes the overdraft and refuses to process the payroll, the church will ask how much of the total payroll can be paid given that 100 per cent of it was paid the month before, and nothing has changed that much since then in terms of income and outgoings. The bank will suggest 90 or 80 per cent and the church will agree: pay them all 80 per cent of their salary. There will be a piece on the *Today* programme and another in the *Daily Telegraph* – it might make 'and finally' on *News at Ten* – but nobody will come up with a better solution and the principle will be entrenched within weeks. Richer parishes will stop paying quota and top up the salaries of their own clergy instead. Poorer parishes will have poorer clergy, some of whom will still see it as their vocation to serve there. Some clergy will leave, easing the pressure on the budget. Those remaining will compete for the higher-paid posts. Within a few years the entire financial system will be half dismantled and half collapsed. The church will have turned financially congregational, with each congregation funding its own minister or ministers or share of a minister. This is no bad conclusion, but it will hardly have been reached by the best of all possible routes.

I set out the financial problems facing the church to one of my former colleagues, suggesting that nobody in the hierarchy was admitting the scale of the problem or doing anything to address it. She reminded me that on the contrary every year brings a new diocesan initiative hoping to turn the situation around. Scratch the surface and behind the endlessly revised presentations these initiatives all have the same objective: to bring in the quota and to manage on ever fewer clergy. The tedious regularity of these initiatives illustrates their failure, as forty-three separate diocesan offices try something different every year and still fail to resolve the crisis or stem the decline.

I ended up serving on a committee designing one of those initiatives to save the diocese in 1999, mostly because I happened to be in the room when the bishop was looking to fill the places. I sat down with a group of high-powered lay people with the task of working out how better to bring in the quota. We addressed some fundamental issues. Most people have no idea how the clergy are funded and just assume they will always be there, like the royal family, the

House of Lords and the village church. And most people have no idea where the quota goes. This latter problem is entirely understandable, as we ourselves were unable to decipher any version of the diocesan accounts. We could find no way to make sense of them. The headings and the entries alike were indecipherable. In the parishes people are challenged to give to God through quota; they deserve better than this. We commissioned one of our number to meet the director of finance and demand to know what was really going on. When we finally worked out where the money was going we realised just how much waste there was, and how different the real picture was from that commonly presented. The parishes were constantly told that the quota funded the parish clergy: in reality a huge proportion went on central diocesan staff and offices, and we were convinced the expenditure on vicarages was three times what it ought to be through sheer inefficiency.

We all knew the solution from the first time we met: let each parish pay its own clergy. There would be a painful process of transition, diocesan office would have to administer it all, but at the end of the day, if people could see a direct connection between payment and result they would be far more likely to pay. In the mean time they were perfectly justified in 'giving to God' in other ways instead.

We thought it too radical to dare to propose, and we assumed it was beyond our remit. We were at cross-purposes with another group meeting simultaneously to save the diocese by changing the way that each parish's individual quota was calculated. It turned out later that they were making a small move in the same direction, but by the time it was implemented it was so thoroughly fudged that nobody noticed the change.

Across a dozen meetings we watered down our proposal to fit the prevailing church culture and our cautious interpretation of the remit. We proposed a separate annual statement for each parish, showing where their particular contribution goes, represented as fractions of a clergyperson and specified support services. After we presented our report the proposal was watered down again at each stage of its processing. Finally some shadow of the idea limped blandly into the public domain to join the long list of failed diocesan initiatives to save the world. I met the chairman of the group again three years later and we both regretted our failure to propose the radical solution the entire group knew to be right from the outset.

In the course of our research for that group we found that the entire transfer of wealth between deaneries – quota's great socialist principle in action – was subsidising just one deanery in the diocese. Newham deanery was receiving a subsidy of £1 million a year from a total budget of £13 million. After decades of annual subsidy at this level the proportion of churchgoers in the Deanery of Newham choosing the Church of England was just 17 per cent, which is less than half the national average. Eighty-three per cent of churchgoers in Newham were choosing a church other than the Church of England: a church with no inter-deanery transfer of funds, a church with no great principle of socialist redistribution, a church where they pay their own clergy out of their own local funds – a church that does not patronise.

Two years later another layman I knew joined the main diocesan finance committee. He found it all quite disturbing for a multi-million-pound organisation. He identified the corporate malaise as fear. Everybody was frightened. In private they knew both the problems and the solutions and would discuss them at length, but once they were in committee if they dared to speak at all they would water it all down to a quarter of what they had imagined. Everybody would cough awkwardly and the committee would water it down three-quarters more. An anodyne motion would be recorded, and in its implementation another three-quarters would be lost. The final impact would be negative: more cost and complexity for no benefit. Everybody was frightened: frightened of making a bad situation worse, frightened of being the one who suggested it, ashamed at the collapse, 'on their watch', of this once-great institution, and desperate to delay financial meltdown by just one more year.

With the financial situation so desperate – and those at the top in each diocese so fearful – those large churches with large quotas have a phenomenal leverage over the leadership. Only a handful have the fundamentalist clergy who could and would persuade their church councils to withhold payment of quota, but a handful is all that it would take to bankrupt a diocese and leave the clergy unpaid. Limited withholdings have begun. Some turn out to be more 'cannot pay' than 'will not pay'; others are fudged as the wealthy parish decides which other parishes it approves sufficiently to subsidise and pays them directly, allowing the diocese to reorder its own funds accordingly. But the precedent is clear: the bishop now does what the fundamentalists say, or the whole diocesan edifice will come crashing down. You do not get much more direct control than that.

And that is why Jeffrey John is not the Bishop of Reading. Resigning 'for the sake of the unity of the church' meant resigning because fundamentalist parishes all over the country were threatening to bankrupt one diocese after another if the appointment went ahead.

My local Roman Catholic priest followed the story as it unfolded in the national media over several weeks in summer 2003. He listened carefully to the arguments on each side until the day he heard the threat to withdraw quota. He wasted no more time listening to the opponents of the appointment. 'They threatened to take away their money. Where is the faith in that? Where is the theology?'

The liberals responded to the threat. Having first approved Jeffrey John's appointment, they now forced him to resign. And where is the faith in that, or the theology?

CHAPTER 11

A Manifesto

It has been a long journey from Henry VIII to today's Church of England, but the church's hierarchy survives intact: the monarch is Supreme Governor, and the forty-three Crown-appointed bishops are permanently endowed. The rest of the church is on the verge of collapse. Attendance is in freefall, the liturgy is in disarray, the bishops are bitterly and publicly divided against each other, and the financial arrangements for nine thousand salaried clergy have become unsustainable.

At the root of the crisis is a structure that pays no heed to the active laity. Even in the system of internal government introduced in 1970 the active laity lose out twice: every baptised person in the country is given the equal right to vote alongside them in the first tier of the synodical system – whether or not they have attended church since their own christening or know anything at all of the church's life and faith – and the elected laity then enter a four-tier system of synodical government (parish, deanery, diocese and nation) that gives the upper hand to the hierarchy in every tier. In all the business that matters there is a veto for the individual incumbent or bishop, or for the House of Clergy or the House of Bishops.

At parish level the vicar chairs the Parochial Church Council, and in virtually every parish sets out the room like a classroom with the teacher's desk at the front. Lay members of the council sit quietly in their rows and come to understand their role as either supporters or opponents of the vicar, who gets his own way in the end regardless. Diocesan synod is like a two-hundred-strong Parochial Church Council. The bishop sits at the front and his senior staff – not parish clergy but his own private entourage – take it in turns across the cycle of meetings to explain their role and significance to the assembly. Members can speak for two minutes, if they must. Only the most politically savvy make it right through the system to the national General Synod, guaranteeing its confrontational nature when it meets residentially twice or three times each year. From the local parish to General Synod the system becomes little more than a forum for timid complaints and political posturing. The real power throughout remains with the hierarchy.

Ordinands are subtly inducted into this culture during the selection and training process by the repeated use of Isaiah chapter 6, the story of the call of the prophet Isaiah. In a godless era God seeks a prophet to go to a godless people, and Isaiah says, 'Here am I, send me.' This is the self-image force-fed to the future clergy: that the clergy have received God's call and responded, and like Isaiah will carry God's message to a godless people. The laity – if not quite godless – are nevertheless clearly defined as the ones who have either rejected God's call or been unfortunate enough never to have received it. It was our universal presumption on ordination day. We expected to keep on moving every few years, carrying God's message to one needy congregation after another. If we were ever to stay in one place for a longer-term ministry it would be in the role of catcher in the rye, pretending to play with the children in the grass while assuming that the children are foolish and in danger and that the catcher alone is capable and wise. It is no wonder the clergy end up addressing their adult congregations – in both content and tone – as if speaking to a room full of children.

The best of the rank and file parish clergy are pulled both ways. They are selected and trained to represent the hierarchy to the laity and they have the obligation and the authority to do so. Most also long to represent the active laity to the hierarchy, but find themselves swimming against the strongest of cultural and constitutional tides. They learn by their own experience that a well-functioning congregation is an egalitarian community, and that a priest needs to work alongside that community with genuine humility. His greatest privilege would be acceptance as a valued part of that community. The Kingdom of God proclaimed by Jesus in the gospels is an egalitarian community where every human being has equality of dignity and worth. The parishes and the best of the clergy know it instinctively and are not well served.

Congregation meetings have no legal status in the Church of England – whose legislation has no concept of 'congregation' – but they have been used informally to great effect as a way of fostering a sense of community and belonging. We used them in Burnley and in Church Langley, and my college contemporaries have used them in cities, towns and villages around the country. Some other denominations have had formal congregation meetings for years and they are as stale as most Parochial Church Councils, but, creatively managed, with seating in the round and time for discussion and feedback, they allow everyone to participate. At first in Church Langley we called them Stay for Lunch Days, with discussion and feedback after the service before a simple shared lunch. Eventually they became our form of government in our own constitution. Each participating denomination retained the right to withdraw from the project – and other checks and balances were in place – but in our ongoing life as a congregation the congregation meeting itself was ultimately sovereign.

In technical terms this is the form of church government known as congregationalism, and it is a concept universally despised throughout the hierarchy of the Church of England. From the local deanery chapter to the House of Bishops it is a token of all that is utterly unacceptable. Any discussion of change in the structures of the church can be brought to a swift close by invoking the term: any proposed change will be rejected unanimously once it has been denounced as congregationalist. Press the point and somebody will intone darkly, 'The church is not a democracy.' Ideally the church is a 'theocracy', with God in charge. In the Church of England, God is assumed to take charge through a divinely ordered hierarchy, an assumption so deeply engrained in the culture at every level that any alternative model is dismissed without so much as a pause. To the intellectual liberals, handing over to the laity smacks of ignorance and populism. To the fundamentalists it looks like an open invitation to error and impurity. To those ordinary working clergy who have found their place in the pecking order it is feared for being the exact opposite of the top-down structure they have come to know and almost trust.

Top-down hierarchical state-sponsored religions like the Church of England have been a unique phenomenon of western Europe for most of the last fifteen hundred years. Nowhere else has religion been quite so micro-managed by secular state authorities for their own political purposes for quite so many years, and nowhere else has religious obser-vance collapsed so dramatically. On a composite scale of religious observance inside and outside the home, the level of religious observance is virtually the same on every conti-nent from the Americas to Japan. The one exception is western Europe, where it has collapsed to one-quarter of the level elsewhere.

The test case has to be the United States: it is a modern western liberal democracy and yet it stands with the rest of the world in maintaining high levels of religious observance. Thirty to forty per cent of the population is in church on any given Sunday morning, compared to less than 5 per cent here. The majority religion is a Christianity exported directly from western Europe, and contrary to transatlantic stereo-type American religion is not all fundamentalism and right-wing political extremism. There is a whole range of lib-eral, progressive and egalitarian denominations thriving in the US, a modern prosperous technological democracy not unlike our own. The defining difference is that two to three hundred years ago every government in western Europe was maintaining a state-sponsored religion as a matter of national pride and banning or persecuting all other practices, while the US was passing the Bill of Rights, enshrining in its own constitution the commitment of the governing authorities neither to promote nor prohibit any religion. Today the outward appearances may be similar – congregations, clergy, church buildings, denominations – but in the US the churches are drawing in a third of the population every weekend, while the churches in western Europe have attendances down below 10 per cent and still in freefall. Church attendance in the US has actually grown over the last two hundred years from a base of around 20 per cent at the time of Independence. The same two-hundred-year period has not been good for the church in western Europe.

For a thousand years the secular powers of western Europe sought control of the churches, and at the reformation they received it. In the United States the governance of the churches belongs not to the secular powers but to the people who choose to organise and then join those churches. There is freedom of religion – a plurality of churches – and the state has a constitutional obligation not to become involved with any of them. The transatlantic contrast is between a continent of monolithic royalist state-sponsored churches and their successors, and a continent that has freedom of religion and the separation of church and state. In the former the churches are in crisis after two hundred years of decline; in the latter the churches continue to draw people in weekend after weekend, representing a larger proportion of the population now than two hundred years ago. The Roman Catholic church worldwide provides a case study in itself. Where it has been the official state-sponsored religion, as in France and Spain, it now struggles, weighed down not only by its political history (the catholic church in France was royalist right into the twentieth century) but by the historic burden of surplus unsuitable buildings. Away from western Europe it is a church of distinctive gathered communities: communities of people freely choosing their faith and allegiance. During the last two hundred years the growth of this church of gathered communities worldwide has confidently outpaced the growth in world population.

The establishment culture of the Church of England also lies behind its current financial crisis. The central deployment of the clergy by the diocese – and the collection of quota to fund that deployment – together form a system of taxation and spending entirely appropriate to a branch of the state. The congregations perceive the diocese as a distant and heavy-handed authority out of touch with parish life. Its quota system and its policies for clergy allocation look arbitrary and unfair. Quota has now reached the level where the parishes are no longer willing or able to pay. The system is unique to the Church of England and has only evolved over the last forty years. It now represents almost the entire income of the church, and under that strain the system is collapsing. The experiment has failed.

The tried and tested system in virtually every other church worldwide – from the Roman Catholic church to the new independent churches – has the clergy paid directly by the congregations they serve. It is a model worth considering for the Church of England. Parishes that are freed from the burden of an artificially inflated quota – subsidising churches they may not wish to endorse anyway – would find a whole range of new and creative opportunities opening up. Smaller parishes that have lost their incumbent in some phase of diocesan redeployment would have the opportunity to plan their own future ministry in voluntary partnership with neighbouring parishes, instead of maintaining a sharing scheme imposed from above. The ordinary one-priest parish would no longer have to keep paying its full quota during a vacancy – an arrangement which has encouraged every diocese to drag its feet over appointments – and for every month the vacancy does continue the parish would find it had the financial opportunity to sort out those disabled access routes, to refurbish the toilets, renew the sound system or install a new kitchen. Having the upper hand financially during the vacancy, the parish would also have more motivation to use its veto over any new appointment – rather than being grateful for any appointment at all – and the end result should be an appointment supported or even selected by the parish, and an altogether healthier relationship between incumbent and congregation. The straightforward financial transparency of the new system could only encourage rather than discourage giving within the church as a whole, and the demise of the much-resented quota and deployment systems might even leave space for some affection for the diocese in its few remaining functions. In order to bring in the quota the church has been telling the active laity for thirty years that 'this is your church,' but the quota and deployment systems have consistently proved the opposite. With direct parish funding of the clergy, the structure begins to match the rhetoric.

The incumbent's security of tenure is being examined at the moment – after the challenge from the European courts – but it will need further reform in favour of the parishes if the new financial arrangements are really to refresh and renew the church. A parish that pays its own priest has to have the ultimate right to say that the appointment is no longer working, and that the time has come for a change.

The church has been battling against the system of private patronage for fifteen hundred years. Patrons' rights have already been curtailed: they now lapse after six months and pass to the bishop if the parish keeps exercising its veto. If a one-clause act to abolish patrons' rights altogether is out of the question, that six-month period should instead be reduced by stages to one month and eventually to nothing – a purely honorary role – encouraging patrons to make themselves genuinely useful as soon as the former incumbent gives notice, or else miss their chance.

Once the parishes are funding their own clergy – it is the only viable solution on the table – they might want to look in some detail at just how much time the clergy spend working on christenings, weddings and funerals for people who have no connection with the church, considering the theological case that much of this work is actively counter-productive, or just the practical case that it might not justify the income it generates (income that will now be diverted to the parish not the diocese). Some parishes will begin to promote the trade as a way of securing an income, encouraging the funeral directors to call their minister first and promoting their venue for weddings and christenings. Other parishes will happily withdraw from that carnival altogether. At present the parish boundary system prevents such local policy-making, requiring clergy to take all christenings, weddings and funerals for residents of their own parish and forbidding them from taking any others. Legislation is already in the system to relax this restriction for weddings, and for christenings and funerals it was only ever a case of culture rather than law. Once we stop inviting every baptised non-churchgoer in the country to vote at their local parish AGM we will be able to abolish the parish boundary concept altogether. At this I hear five thousand territorial incumbents shudder, and nine hundred thousand churchgoers shrug with indifference. More than half of all Church of England churchgoers cross a parish boundary to go to church on Sunday morning. Even with our deliberately local focus in Church Langley, more than half our congregation was coming in from outside the area.

Those most afraid of the new system will be the clergy, who will find out for the first time whether their congregations actually value them or not. The best should thrive. The rest might take more trouble to keep up to date with their training opportunities, their annual retreats and their daily prayers, and focus full-time on building up the congregation rather than ruling their patch like a local baron. It is possible that a handful of the worst might drop out of the system, but this is no worse than the present arrangement, where it is a high proportion of the best.

The new system will invite congregations to think creatively about their priorities. Each congregation will determine for itself how to divide up its resources between buildings, clergy, and other projects and causes. Some will abandon their remaining eighth of a clergy-person and transform seamlessly into building-preservation trusts. Others will hand over the keys of their buildings to English Heritage and move on, perhaps gathering in larger groups elsewhere in bright modern or modernised buildings with whole teams of excellent staff. We will finally have the church of the active laity, liberated from the baggage of its history, with solutions no longer imposed from above but chosen by the congregations themselves: the church finally becomes the church of the people.

Gathering in larger groups means bringing two or more congregations together, and in the divided Church of England that can look like a near-impossible task, but the high water mark for the unity and confidence and integrity of the Church of England was the ASB era, the era that produced my own generation of young ordinands. A commitment to the ideal of unity served us well in ministry, and has to be part of the vision for the future church despite everything.

Church Langley Church began as the unlikely joint project of an anglo-catholic parish and a local baptist church, and it worked for everyone. For the Church of England service we used the bare essentials of the mass, adding a mixture of hymns old and new. We agreed from the outset that there would be Church of England Sundays and Baptist Sundays – rather than some bland, negotiated and constraining weekly compromise – as long as there was communion in some form, and encouraging the use of the set readings. As the months went by the two forms of service converged to become virtually identical, because we were growing together and becoming one community.

The future dream would be to bring half a dozen or more Church of England congregations, or even congregations of mixed denomination, into dialogue, to create again that united utopia: simple dignified modern catholic liturgy, and a congregational culture and structure, in a bright modern or modernised building for a new congregation hundreds strong.

It is not just that a larger congregation can do more, offering a wide range of liturgies and activities throughout the week: a larger congregation is also a fundamentally different kind of Christian community. With our ever-smaller gatherings we are not so much offering congregations as clubs. Anyone walking in through the door of a typical Church of England church has to do so on the basis that everybody present will know they are new. In a larger congregation they have the opportunity to be anonymous observers for a while if they wish, and equally the opportunity to become more involved, in their own time, through the wide range of other liturgies and activities on offer. Seventy is a key number for communities: below seventy, everybody can and will know everybody else; above seventy, a variety of different networks emerges. The Church of England has become almost uniform in offering congregations of fewer than seventy, intimate clubs for the minority of people who like that kind of thing. Congregations of more than seventy are large and diverse organisations with a place for everyone. In the teaching of Saint Paul, the local church represents the whole church: all the gifts of the universal church are present in the diversity of the local congregation. To begin to make that vision a reality you probably need at least seventy committed adults gathered together in one place. I suspect that anything less is not really a church, despite its building and its priest.

A pattern of large and thriving congregations might have developed naturally, but the Church of England has actively intervened to prevent it. Increasingly over the last forty years, through the quota and clergy allocation systems, the church has taken resources away from the larger congregations and used them to provide an artificial subsidy for the smaller congregations. Larger congregations struggle under an unsustainable burden of quota, with too few clergy for the task in hand, while their funds and clergy are allocated to congregations that are too small to be viable. The church has been robbing the active present to preserve the structures of the past.

Buildings are a major issue for the contemporary church. A decent campus for a modern congregation should be a top-quality modern public building, light, open and accessible, with the liturgical space arranged so that everybody feels part of the main event, close to the scriptures and close to the altar. Pillars, pews and long thin buildings are unhelpful, and the classic Church of England bottleneck of choir stalls excludes the entire congregation from the main event. When congregations take the bold decision to combine – in order to gather in larger groups – the options will be to redevelop an existing site to a decent modern standard or to build something entirely new. Some of the old buildings may justify the investment for the sake of the period features that can be retained in a fully redeveloped property, but just as often the constraints of cost and the state of the existing building will make it preferable to begin again with a site and building entirely new.

There are already surplus buildings no longer required for regular liturgical use, and when congregations begin to gather in larger groups there will be more. Many of them are in poor condition, unfit for any contemporary use: after being photographed for the archives they should be demolished and the sites sold. Others are in a worthwhile state of repair and could be sold for alternative commercial uses: office space, leisure facilities or residential development. Some represent 'heritage' to varying degrees: existing planning and listed building laws should provide the degree of protection appropriate to each. Where this leaves a building with neither liturgical function nor commercial value, a parish should hand over the keys to the authorities and walk away.

The more ancient and the more rural present the greater problem. Where the church has no further use for a building, but the wider population wishes to see that building preserved, it is for the wider population, not the church, to bring that preservation about. English Heritage and the National Trust can have as many as they wish. The hotels that now dominate the commercial wedding industry would be glad to take some as wedding chapels, and local building-preservation trusts will emerge to protect others. If the whole population of a village wishes to support its historic building they can adopt it through their local council, funding its preservation through local taxation. If the will is not sufficient to keep the building safe and secure the alternative to preservation is the redevelopment of the site as an attractive public garden with interesting historic features: you dismantle the building and plant flowers in what remains. The church is not dead: it is further down the valley, open and active all week, with a large campus, a huge car park and a Sunday congregation of a thousand. It might even be choosing to contribute to the upkeep of some of those ancient holy sites.

There has been just one experiment in congregational

government inside the structures of the Church of England itself. In creating the option known as Resolution C the Church of England stumbled accidentally into its first major experiment in serious congregational empowerment. Resolutions A and B were negative – declining the services of a female priest or vicar – but Resolution C offered a positive choice: to opt into a new network of parishes, complete with its own bishops to co-ordinate their common life. While priest and people in any given parish were generally in agreement in making the move, the legislation gave the power to the people, not to the priest. They were empowered to make a positive choice that made a highly significant difference to their life as a church, and they thrived in the simple knowledge that they could make it, unmake it and remake it at will. The responsibilities of significant decision-making had finally arrived for the laity of the Church of England.

The Church of England has had its first serious taste of congregationalism and the world has not come to an end. There is one remaining anomaly for those parishes: while they have exercised their right to choose their own bishop and network, they remain subject to their old diocese with its quota-based financial system and in its policies for clergy allocation. The Resolution C churches should now be the first to be set free from local diocesan control and allowed to manage their own resources, whether as individual congregations or as a network. It will resolve many resentments and battles of will.

Where different factions are trapped within a single organisation, the whole operation can be paralysed by mutual suspicion and battles for control. A formal division into separate organisations ends the mutual obsession and allows each group to operate without wasting energy on internal strife. Each new organisation can then thrive or decline on its own merits. Mutual respect – even new co-operation – may develop.

It happened to the parish in Harlow. Mistrust emerged between the old church (Saint Mary Magdalene) and the new church (Church Langley Church) – worsening rapidly when the vicar moved on and the post was vacant for a while. The old church became fearful that everything it loved might change. In two key elections that year – for the Parochial Church Council and for the two parish representatives who would hold one veto each over the new appointment – not a single member of the new church was elected. The new church was left entirely subject to the old, with no say at all in its own management. Mutual suspicion and battles for control would have crippled both churches if they had been forced to co-exist as one parish for years on end. Instead the parish was divided in two, and both sides promptly flourished. The old church took a look at itself, stood tall and voted itself into the Resolution C network of traditionalist parishes. The new church 'came of age' and established congregational structures for its own ongoing life. Both have gone from strength to strength with clarity of vision and purpose.

The Church of England nationally is paralysed by factionalism, and the solution is the same: a formal division to bring to an end the mutual obsession and the battles for control. Resolution C has established the model and demonstrated its effectiveness. Now we need resolutions D, E, F, G, H, J and K. It is time for the self-appointed leaders of the various factions to stop playing politics in high places and set out their agendas for the congregations to decide. The traditionalist anglo-catholics have done it to great effect, and now it is time for the evangelicals and others to take up the same challenge. The evangelicals themselves are far from united: the harsh fundamentalism of Reform is different from the dry protestantism of the Evangelical Alliance and different again from the leadership-obsessed post-charismatic New Wine network or the Sunday-supplement glossiness of Alpha. It is time for an open and honest debate about what each faction believes and why, and the implications for individuals and the future of the church. Required to give straight answers to some basic questions, the leaders of the various factions may find the laity – and the grass-roots clergy – less sympathetic to their strident agendas than they presumed.

The new networks should set out their agendas and the congregations should decide. Given three or four years' notice, the networks will have time to evolve into forms the congregations will welcome or at the very least accept. If the congregations are unimpressed by the offers on the table they will have time to set up alternative networks of their own.

The new resolutions should not be resolutions to opt out, as Resolution C has been. If anything is left behind out of which to opt, the liberals and the fundamentalists will fight for control of that vestigial mainstream just as they do now. The 'do-nothing' option should allow a congregation to retain its current vicar but would offer no bishop or synod or network. As the years go by each network can thrive or falter on its merits as the laity make their choice.

The new networks will mean the end of the present

paralysed structures of control at the diocesan and national level. At the local level the ecumenical clergy fraternal replaces the old deanery chapter. The clergy can also meet for some genuine collegiality with clergy of the same network across a slightly larger area, as the clergy of Resolution C already do. Some of the networks will elect bishops while others will manage without. Some will try to centralise their funding while others will keep it local. Some may welcome in congregations from other denominations – one at a time or in great merger schemes – but it will always be for the congregations to decide. And each new network in turn will do what a well-functioning denomination is supposed to do: act as both a voluntary association of congregations and a professional association of clergy, set and maintain standards, give direction and purpose, and provide such services and compile such resources as the congregations commission from time to time.

A whole range of new networks could emerge. There might be a civic churches' network, for churches whose primary self-image is a seamless integration with the local Institute and Civic Society, where the mayor pays a formal visit with his chain of office every year and flags hang in the sanctuary. There might be a choral churches' network, for those places where the choir rules the roost. There might be some kind of liberal or radical churches' network, where justice campaigns take the lead and sacraments and creeds are way down the list. There will probably be a 'just as anglo-catholic as you' network for congregations that have embraced the ordination of women but still like their formal processions, incense, tunicles, fiddle-backs and apparelled amices. Their particular tragedy is that they are as many decades behind contemporary Roman

Catholicism as the congregations of Resolution C, the reforms of the Second Vatican Council having passed them by in their anglo-catholic isolation.

Many of us will be aiming for the simple modern catholicism we knew in the united era of ASB, inclusive enough in Church Langley to embrace baptist and catholic alike. The question is how to describe who we are, and what name to give our new network.

'Catholic' is a difficult word to use in England. From the beginning of the reformation era it better served the purposes of protestant monarchs and parliaments and churchmen to maintain a mythology of Roman Catholic conspiracy, immorality and error than to spread the news of the reforms emanating from the Council of Trent. The consequence is that anti-catholic prejudice remains perniciously steadfast wherever protestant parliaments or monarchs prevailed. I still meet otherwise sensible protestant leaders who consider it an article of faith that they must oppose Roman Catholicism and all its works. There is an idle assumption that nothing much of interest happened between the resurrection and the beginning of the reformation, and that nothing has changed in the Roman Catholic church since 1517. Even amongst protestants who welcome dialogue with Roman Catholics there is a patronising assumption that the catholic church is full of pre-reformation 'errors' and will never quite 'catch up with the rest of us'. In reclaiming the word catholic we challenge all that prejudice.

Unfortunately the word catholic is used by other groups within the Church of England, including both the traditionalists of Resolution C and the liberals – previously liberal catholics – who are now drifting, bewildered and apologetic, in the direction of evangelical fundamentalism. If the word is to be used it needs a qualifying adjective. The word 'modern' might have served – modern catholic in the spirit of the Second Vatican Council and ASB – but the word sounds dated in a 'post-modern' world. An alternative might be the word 'progressive', with its sense of forward movement: a work in progress, a people on a pilgrimage. In the context of six continents and twenty centuries, 'progressive catholic' may not be a bad description of who we are. In all the best moments of its history the Church of England has been a refreshed and renewed version of the catholic faith. For the noticeboard and the letterhead I imagine: 'Saint Luke's Catholic Church, part of the Progressive Catholic Network'. A footnote can explain the details.

Our closest ecumenical partner will be the Roman Catholic church, renewed and refreshed by the reforms of the Second Vatican Council. The unique heritage of the Church of England has been its fusion of elements both catholic and protestant: the Church of England is a minor player in global Christianity but it occupies a unique position between a billion Roman Catholics on one side and half a billion protestants on the other. Global protestantism is now dominated by evangelicalism, and evangelicalism by fundamentalism: by naming the Roman Catholic church as our closest ecumenical partner we distance ourselves from the current Church of England drift towards protestant fundamentalism and claim a place instead alongside the global Christian majority. The Roman Catholic church today has more adherents than all other Christian denominations combined. In terms of Sunday attendance it is the largest church even in England, larger than the Church of England and more united as well. It keeps good liturgy, takes the scriptures seriously rather than idolising them, and in the UK benefits from decent-sized congregations and appropriate modern buildings. John Paul II maintained an ideological pacifism, led unprecedented inter-faith moves, and found a way to apologise with dignity for the historic errors of the church. *The Catechism of the Catholic Church*, published under his leadership in 1992, manages to be simultaneously accessible, thorough and profound: on every one of its eight hundred pages it shows up the vacuous nature of the Church of England's attempts at theology, even the three-year residential version at a respected Church of England theological college in the late 1980s. The only points of significant disagreement with that document – a predictable list including contraception and the all-male, all-celibate priesthood – are matters that Paul VI refused to allow the Second Vatican Council to consider. A Third Vatican Council could resolve them all, given the private views of virtually all Catholic bishops, priests and lay people. It might take a Fourth Vatican Council to work through the authority issues; the pope is currently elected for life by his predecessors' appointees, controls all other appointments in the church, and signs edicts drafted by powerful Vatican insiders who appear to remain instinctively reactionary generation after generation. The Progressive Catholic Network could establish its own egalitarian culture and structure, hold true to the reforming spirit of the Second Vatican Council, and find its own local solutions to those problems that still hold back the Roman church. It will become an expression of the refreshed and renewed catholicism that has defined all that has been best in the Church of England from the beginning.

Global evangelicalism, in contrast, remains fixed in the theology of the sixteenth century, with its wrathful and condemning God and its brutal transaction to buy his appeasement. It has little time for openness, mystery or silence. Catholicism lives contentedly with mystery; it uses the word to describe the sacraments: the holy mysteries. It recognises instinctively that there are truths and experiences too profound and too beautiful for words, the truths that we encounter and contemplate in the silence.

The charismatic movement in those early days had the silence and the space to experience those truths that are too profound and too beautiful for words. It had wonder, reverence, anticipation, and the sense of an awesome God on the move into places yet unknown. It welcomed and celebrated some mystery. From the fifth *Songs of Fellowship* LP in 1980: 'You've left so many questions still unanswered: you're such a mystery.' From the sixth in 1981: 'Your love for me is a mystery.' In the days of its folk-movement authenticity the charismatic movement had space for God to be the God of 'Love Unknown'. It could recognise the profound spirituality in the life of prayer of a convent sister. It could meditate on the suffering of Christ for its own sake, as a meditation on the mystery of the incarnation, not a theory of salvation. And whilst the language was individual – about being 'born again' and 'filled with the spirit' – the experience was of belonging: belonging to a movement that was sharing a new experience of God, and belonging to a fellowship of intimate trust and mutual commitment. It was a truly catholic spirituality lost and adrift. It was netted by protestant evangelicalism before it could find its way back home.

Once the new networks are in place – with their own bishops, clergy, structures, policies, liturgies and life – there will not be much of a role remaining for an umbrella body called the Church of England. It might find a role as an employment agency for a while, managing the payroll on behalf of the networks and the congregations, but the networks and the congregations could manage this perfectly well on their own in time. It will survive more significantly as a land-management body: a state quango, as indeed it is now. There will be complex issues to resolve about who owns all those historic buildings: who has the right to use them and the duty to maintain them, whether grants will be made or rent charged or leases and freeholds transferred. I am sure this will generate plenty of work for those who currently occupy the corridors of power, perhaps even enough to retain some of those forty-three redundant regional offices. This Church of England Residuary Body will have to have secular state-appointed trustees: the last thing we need is to have rival religious parties battling for its control. The management of land and buildings will be all that it does, for that will be all that remains, and when a congregation leaves one of those ancient buildings for a more appropriate new site of its own, it will leave the old institution behind for good.

One of the greatest gifts of the reformation era was some excellent theological work on the nature of the church and what it means to be a part of it. In established churches this work was lost, as membership of church and nation was once again conflated. This is the Church of England's inheritance: it has no theology of the laity. The proper recognition of the laity was preserved in the minority churches around Europe, especially the Baptist and Congregational churches. It also became the single most powerful theme in the theology of the Second Vatican Council. From the 1960s onwards, protestant and catholic theology alike celebrate the biblical ideals of every member ministry and the priesthood of all believers.

With such egalitarian ideals, we might wonder whether a separate ordained ministry is justified at all. Certainly protestant theology has always struggled with the concept, and the 1992 *Catechism of the Catholic Church* speaks so fully and so richly of the common priesthood of all the faithful that the section on ordained ministry jars when it comes around.

The classic Church of England understanding of holy orders involves an ontological change (a change in the status of being), like a permanent branding on the individual soul of the person being ordained. The clergy are welded into a hierarchy that begins with Jesus, Saint Peter and the apostles and continues, by a physical link of ordaining hands placed on ordinands' heads, down to every validly ordained person in the world today. The clergy have had the ontological change, and the laity have not. This model turns out to be more an anglican chip on anglican shoulders than the preservation of a catholic ideal: it is central to the anglo-catholic claim to have valid catholic orders in the apostolic succession, despite the break with Rome. The Roman Catholic church itself sits light to the concept: if you marry or cease to say mass or disobey your bishop you cease to be a priest for all practical purposes, although they will not bother to ordain you again if you change your mind and they agree to take you back. There is also an important nuance lost in translation. In the early texts the church does not have holy orders for individuals, but holy order for itself. The individuals set apart by that ordering are no more holy as individuals than the laity, they just have particular roles within the one holy ordering of the whole church.

On this understanding of holy order, there is the potential for holy order in any church or denomination on its own terms, and no holy order at all in the fundamentally disordered Church of England. For all practical purposes there has been no mutual recognition of ministries between Church of England congregations of different traditions for at least a hundred years. No evangelical vicar would allow an anglo-catholic priest anywhere near his pulpit or altar, and if an anglo-catholic church ever allowed an evangelical in it would be with gritted teeth, rolling eyes and reluctant magnanimity. It would never occur to the contemporary fundamentalists to place any value on anglican ordination in determining who is worthy to lead, speak or minister. The attitude of the liberals is ultimately the same, as they wince at news from the evangelical and anglo-catholic extremes and try to retain some comfortable space in the centre ground. The vicarage clergy think little of the Church of England's part-time Non-Stipendiary Ministers and Ordained Local Ministers, and even amongst the stipendiary the difference between the beneficed and the non-beneficed is far more significant than the difference between lay and ordained. For all practical purposes none of these people actually believes in anglican orders. We do better to wipe the slate clean and begin again, seeking holy order amongst fellow Christians as equals before God and in fellowship one with another. Within the priesthood of all believers, most go out at the end of the service to be the active priesthood in the outside world. Those who stay on in church are their support and resource staff. The laity are primary, the clergy are secondary. The bishops, if we choose to have them at all, are even further removed than that.

In the ideally ordered church there would be professional training and qualifications, and a professional body maintaining standards. The clergy would not be regarded as any more holy than the rest of the population. Their homes would not be regarded as public property: they would have the same right to private time and private space as everyone else. The expectations would be realistic: no single individual can be there for everybody all of the time. They would be professional people doing the work for which they had been trained like any other professional: called by God and the people to be pastors in the church where others have been called by God and the people to their various roles; and the value of each role is equal, neither greater nor less.

These competent professional pastors would not be the ruthlessly efficient managers and hard-nosed leaders demanded by the contemporary culture of the Church of England for its few remaining stipendiary posts. They would be theologically literate from the outset, continually studying the sacred texts of the faith, steeped in the scriptures, study and prayer. They would look after their own spiritual health as athletes look after their physical health. They would co-ordinate the life of the congregation on behalf of all its members. They would help the congregation to reflect on the scriptures in the light of contemporary life, and vice versa, offering homilies in the liturgy and courses for study and dialogue. They may even be available at designated times for private consultation, if you booked an appointment through the office as you would with any other professional.

At the heart of their work would be their responsibility for the daily and weekly liturgy of the church. In this they would participate with neither method-actor intensity nor light-entertainment levity, but with adult-to-adult ordinariness, as one amongst equals and all equal before God.

Most people can change a fuse, treat a headache, plumb in a new washing machine, jump-start a car, perhaps even change the spark plugs, fix a washer, give emergency first aid or wire in a new socket, but we still need electricians, doctors, plumbers and mechanics who maintain, develop and pass on the knowledge of each profession. We do not need them often or for everything, but there is value and order in having them there. Anybody can offer Christian advice and prayer, but there is value and order in having some who are devoted to its study and service as their full-time vocation.

In the Baptist tradition at Church Langley Church it was accepted without question that a lay person could preside at communion as validly as any other minister, although as a matter of good order you would not invite just anybody who walked in off the street. From our sponsoring Baptist church we inherited the practice that only those on the elected representative body for the congregation could lead holy communion, and that in discussion amongst themselves not all would wish to do so. On this basis a Baptist layman from the Baptist church regularly led services and led them well. By stages he moved over from the old church to the new church and became a highly valued part of our common life. We adopted into our own constitution the right of lay people elected to our own representative body to lead services of holy communion, as long as they were not members of the Church of England (to keep us within Church of England rules). The arrangement was only ever used to reauthorise the same person, now repeatedly top of the annual ballot. Then we realised that the clause requiring all those elected to take a break one year in seven meant the authorisation would shortly be suspended for a year, so we amended the constitution again to create the post of 'lay pastor' under the authority of the Baptist minister, and unanimously appointed him to the post. This is how we ordered ourselves, creating and maintaining our own holy order.

The obsession with hierarchy and the ontological change, and the absence of any theology of the laity, have led the Church of England into a muddle of licensed lay ministries and non-stipendiary and ordained local ministries, where some have supposedly had the ontological change and others have not, the relationship with role and training has become confused to the point of disorder, and clerical collars and titles have become symbols of hierarchy, privilege and pride. In the new networks we will do better to wipe the slate clean and begin again, with no chips on shoulders and a spirit of mutual respect and servanthood. It will be far more important to work out a half-decent theology of the laity, alongside a practical holy order for the network and for each congregation, than to concern ourselves with any theory of ontological change.

Some will ask whether this new network of networks is 'anglican', but the word no longer has any meaning. The Church of England is in disarray and the worldwide Anglican Communion is worse, a monster created in our own image two and three hundred years ago when we divided up the world amongst our several highly partisan missionary societies. Those who love all the best that anglicanism has been should look on with pride rather than sadness as it spawns a dozen new creative denominations, taking forward all that has been good, and escaping from the dead-end into which the Church of England has been shunted this last dozen years. Taking their place amongst the other UK and European denominations, they may finally create the kind of vibrant church scene that has served the US so well since before Independence.

The final disestablishment of the church may leave the lawyers pondering for decades. The existence of a national church is assumed in the unwritten British constitution, not least at the coronation of a monarch. An adequate vestige of a national church might be just those Crown-appointed bishops and nothing else, perhaps reduced in number from forty-three to the traditional top five, and even those reduced to merely honorary titles equivalent to life peerages or OBEs. Working out the details need not delay the introduction of the new disestablished regime for nine thousand clergy and sixteen thousand congregations. For the sake of the future church it is time to disestablish and dismantle what remains of the ancient Church of England.

EPILOGUE

The move from my first post in Burnley to my second in Church Langley catapulted me through sixty years in a day. The north of England still has a culture of local identity and local history, particularly pronounced in a market town like Burnley, in a valley of the Industrial Revolution. I regularly conducted funerals in Burnley for people who had lived in the same terraced street since they were born. Burnley knew the Second World War was over, but not much of significance had happened since then. Groups of teenagers would address me as Father in the street. Church life, home life and work life were comfortable. Things have moved on just a little since then. Soon after I left in 1993, factory closures and race riots dragged Burnley into the late 1970s.

If Burnley was thirty years behind the curve, Church Langley was thirty years ahead of it. Everyone in the new parish had arrived since 1992, a third from across Harlow, a third from the M11 corridor from east London to Cambridge, and a third from anywhere in the country as people were looking for a home near the M25. There was no history. Everything was new. Most of the men set foot on the ground only on their own driveway, between the car and the front door. The women would supplement this with the gap between Tesco and the school, at opposite ends of the same large car park. Within a year they might as easily be in Basildon, Reading, Liverpool, Thurrock or Slough: people who have recently moved house are more likely, not less, to move house again soon. We once lost a third of our enrolled membership to house moves in just two years. The majority in Church Langley were third generation 'unchurched', and often chillingly materialistic. Church was a sanctuary in the midst of it all, building a sense of community and belonging.

Those we gathered in to become Church Langley Church were almost uniformly evangelical: so much of the rest of the church has been moribund for so many years. And yet we ended up building our life around a modern catholic liturgy and a progressive theology. Evangelicalism offers distinctiveness and commitment, but there remains a hunger unsatisfied. We broke the bread of heaven each time we met and sought communion with our generous God in the stillness and the silence, as well as in the music that made you move your feet. Nobody could pigeonhole us. We were doing something wholesome and new.

The best moment of the week was ten to ten on Sunday morning. There was a tangible sense of gathering anticipation that the unmissable weekly event was about to begin. We had ten minutes of music before the formal liturgy began at ten, reviving those 1970s worship songs, some classic hymns and a handful of more modern items: we worshipped as we gathered. The hospitality team would be completing the preparation of refreshments in the kitchen, the welcome team would be greeting people at the door, the duty sacristan would be arranging two lay deacons to serve at the altar and two chalice bearers to assist with the distribution of communion. I would already have rehearsed the responsorial psalm with the musicians, three other scripture readers would be checking the readings at the lectern, the intercessor for the day would be collecting slips of paper from those requesting specific prayers, and the whole gathering would be moving resolutely towards the moment when it would all begin.

The use of those old worship songs spread spontaneously to the distribution of communion. The musicians played in the background and people joined in, so we made it a feature. To listen to our service, or to read the long list of hymn numbers printed out like a classic hymnboard and fixed to the wall, you might have thought we were just another informal post-charismatic fellowship, but the moment the liturgy began at ten it was pure modern catholic, unfolding like a dance in which everyone knew the moves. As more lay people became involved I could sit out more and the liturgy would happen around me. I was there not as sole performer but as co-ordinator of ministries within the priesthood of all believers.

At the most sacred moments of the service all eyes would be fixed on the sacraments. 'This is my body, which is given for you. This is my blood of the new covenant. Behold the Lamb of God.' We sang the congregational parts around the eucharistic prayer, and on special occasions I would sing the whole prayer: one vulnerable, unaccompanied voice, and profound Christian mysteries. It was music that created intimacy, not distance, as I stood at the central altar and the people were gathered around on all sides. They were the glory days. When I speak to despondent clergy I recall those days. This is how it could be.

At our weekly Bible-study mass one Tuesday evening in 2003, someone deliberately raised the question of the ongoing argument about whether Jeffrey John should proceed to be Bishop of Reading. It was a bold move, but she knew what she was doing: that this was a church where people could speak and listen openly rather than mumble with embarrassment or take a stance. I listened as one by one, from different perspectives, each of those present made their defence of the appointment: those who had the duty to seek God's will had chosen him; only God can know people's hearts; none of us is in a position to judge; he has a valuable and fruitful ministry; he is scholarly and knows the scriptures better than any of us ever will. And one, in the evolving spirit of Church Langley Church, had looked up the topic in the catholic catechism, which she quoted accurately and with authority: homosexual Christians 'must be accepted with respect, compassion and sensitivity'. The lay people have moved on while the leaders squabble.

Regrets, I have a few. I wish I had spent more of the last three years at Church Langley telling people that what we were doing was essentially modern catholicism. I bit my tongue for the sake of the anti-catholic prejudice that is rife in English culture generally and in evangelical and free-church culture in particular. It is hard to say what you value if you do not know its name.

Five or six years into the Church Langley project I visited my home town. I looked down from the high vantage point of the castle in the middle of town. Way down below hymns were being sung in the town centre. I knew it had to be either Saint James's or the new church that emerged after the closure of the Friday-night fellowship. I headed for the marketplace.

I recognised half of them despite all the years. Brian, the old fellowship leader, was in the front row. Myrtle his wife was standing by a prayer-requests desk, a fashionable out-reach technique for a few years in the late 1990s. At the end of a hymn, Brian and a few others came over to greet me. How to sum up fifteen years in a sentence? I said I was the Church of England minister for a new church on a new estate, three and a half thousand homes on a greenfield site. I talked about the new building and the new congregation and quoted some statistics. 'Very good, very good, must get back.' I listened to another half a song and left, as I was only in town for a few hours more.

Over the next few days I regretted the shallow emptiness of the news I had shared. All I really wanted to tell Brian was that, after all these years, God was still my number one passion every hour of every day, God as Creator and Saviour and Spirit, leading the adventure of faith. I turned the experience into a sermon that weekend. 'Compared to that you can keep the new building, keep the new church, even keep the ordination. Take it all away. All that matters is to keep on loving this Jesus through every hour of every day.'

The challenge to the church is to proclaim that faith afresh in each generation.

GLOSSARY

Alpha Course

The Alpha Course is a fifteen-part seminar series created in the mid-1980s at Holy Trinity, Brompton, introducing the basics of **evangelical charismatic** culture and teaching. It was repackaged as a mass-market product in the early 1990s, with the talks available on video and in book form. The recommended programme for each seminar includes a meal and discussion in small groups. The promoters also recommend a day away to cover two of the three seminars on the Holy Spirit – the Alpha Holy Spirit Day. There is nothing new in the basic structure of the course: informal discussion groups, structured introductions to the essentials of the faith and even themed days away have all been used in parishes for centuries. Alpha's contribution is the populist marketing and branding of the format, combined with a clear party line on every issue. As a result, Alpha has become the biggest single vehicle for the promotion of evangelical charismatic culture within the Church of England and the UK's mainstream and independent **protestant** churches. According to the project's communications director, more than 1.6 million people have now attended the course in the UK, in more than seven thousand different churches. Cinema and bus advertising has supplemented church advertising to produce a brand recognition rating of 14 per cent in the mainstream UK population. The course is promoted as being intended 'primarily for non-churchgoers and new Christians'. In reality churches use the brand name to identify themselves with the culture of the course, then either use the official videos or do their own thing under the fifteen seminar headings – and most of those attending are already committed churchgoers. If Alpha had produced 1.6 million new churchgoers over the last ten years church attendance would have almost doubled, and clearly it has not: its promoters spin a mythology about the nature and role of the course that is not reflected in the reality on the ground. Other research suggests that more people drop out of the course than finish it: if this is the case, Alpha could even be driving people away from the church at the very point at which they are most interested in joining.

Alternative Service Book 1980 (ASB)

A compilation of modern-language services authorised for use in the Church of England from 1980 onwards as alternatives to the services in the **Book of Common Prayer**. ASB was withdrawn from use in the year 2000 and replaced by a rambling collection of texts known collectively as *Common Worship*.

Anglican/Anglican Communion

The adjective Anglican means of or relating to the Church of England. The Anglican Communion is a worldwide network of national or regional churches with historic links to the Church of England. Over the last 150 years most of these churches have become increasingly autonomous, making the Anglican Communion a network of autonomous regional churches, although all still look to the Archbishop of Canterbury as first among equals in the network. Since 1888 there has been an agreed statement of what it means to be Anglican: recognition of the scriptures and the **creeds**, the practice of **baptism** and holy communion, and a church structure that includes bishops. For most of its history since then the Church of England has been **liberal catholic,** and the liberal catholic Episcopal Church of the USA has been a leading player in the Anglican Communion, so the word Anglican has carried a liberal catholic nuance. With increasing autonomy for the national churches (in parallel with the decline of the British Empire) the Anglican Communion became less relevant, and was held together by an informal gathering of all the world's Anglican bishops once every ten years. In the late twentieth century, however, these gatherings began to act increasingly like a legislative council, even though they had no formal authority over the various churches of the Communion: they presumed to declare policies on global issues (such as favouring the use of arms in liberation struggles), and to comment on developments in different autonomous regions of the Communion (such as the **ordination** of women). The logical conclusion of this development was conflict between member churches of the Communion. This came to a head at the most recent conference, in 1998. The evangelical George Carey was chairing the conference in his role as Archbishop of Canterbury. A classic **liberal** compromise motion on homosexuality, prepared by the Human Sexuality Study Group, was replaced in full session by a highly partisan fundamentalist-inspired motion presented by the African Issues Group, presuming to lay down the law on the subject for the entire Communion. The liberals thought the text was ambiguous enough to work around, but the fundamentalists had had their moment of triumph and the ramifications are still being worked out. In managing the ongoing dispute, Rowan Williams (Archbishop of Canterbury since 2002) could have pointed to the existing principle of provincial autonomy within an informal federation of national churches, but instead has strengthened the structures of the Communion: the Communion is becoming less a network of autonomous churches and more a single global denomination with global policies. Its first clear global policy is that it is against homosexuality, and disciplinary action has been taken against the churches of Canada and the United States, which at the time of writing have both been excluded from all Anglican Communion business. Nigeria is now demanding action against England, for permitting its clergy to enter celibate civil partnerships. In less than ten years the Anglican Communion has gone from being a network of liberal catholic informality to being a highly organised promoter of global **fundamentalism**, with the elimination of homosexuals from the church its first major policy initiative. At the moment, in classic form, the fundamentalists repeatedly threaten to walk away unless their new demands are met, and the liberals meet every new demand 'for the sake of unity'. Total membership of Anglican Communion churches – excluding non-church-going English people – is below fifty million, more than half of whom are in Nigeria and Uganda.

Anglo-catholic

Classically the **catholic** influence within the Church of England, which has held together both catholic and **protestant** influences since the time of the **reformation**. The 'anglo' prefix is regarded as slightly patronising, as it suggests that anglo-catholics are something other than proper catholics: anglo-catholics prefer to think of themselves simply as catholics who happen to worship in the Church of England, and like to think of the Church of England as a catholic church, with its continuous line of bishops back to the reformation and beyond; they resent the assumption of the **Roman Catholic** church and others that only Roman Catholics are real catholics. The status of anglo-catholicism has changed significantly since the **ordination** of women as priests in the Church of England. Anglo-catholics opposing the ordination of women became a distinct separatist faction for the first time, rather than an informal party or influence, increasingly alienated from the Church of England mainstream, which in their view is no longer catholic. Anglo-catholics supporting the ordination of women remain within the Church of England mainstream, but find themselves so outnumbered by **evangelicals** that they are unable to maintain a significant catholic influence.

The result is an increasingly uniform protestant and evangelical culture within the Church of England.

Archdeacon

A senior priest, appointed by and answerable to a diocesan **bishop,** who may or may not have his or her own **parish** as well, who looks after a range of practical matters across approximately fifty or a hundred parishes, especially concerning staff and buildings.

Area bishop

A junior **bishop,** appointed by and answerable to a diocesan bishop, with delegated bishop's responsibilities for a specific area of a large **diocese.**

Baptism

A public ceremony in which the person being baptised is briefly submerged in water, or has water sprinkled symbolically over them. The ceremony is the mark of membership of the Christian church. All mainstream churches recognise each others' baptism, with the exception of Baptist churches, which do not recognise sprinkling or the baptism of children too young to speak for themselves. Most Church of England churches have a stone font large enough for the submersion of an infant: sprinkling is only for the sickly in the 1662

Book of Common Prayer. Churches regularly practising adult baptism by full submersion often have a section of floor that lifts to reveal a tank large enough for the purpose. Alternatively they may use a collapsible above-ground tank, or hire a swimming pool, or use a natural open-air location such as a lake, a river or the sea.

Baptist

A **protestant denomination** defined by its rejection of the **baptism** of infants in favour of the baptism only of persons old enough to speak for themselves, usually understood as teenagers and adults only. Baptist churches count the baptism of infants as invalid, and so will baptise teenagers or adults who have been previously baptised as infants, the practice known pejoratively as anabaptism or rebaptism. Behind this clearly identifiable practice lies a theology of the importance of each individual and their personal commitment to the faith and the church. Consequently authority structures in Baptist churches are **congregational** rather than hierarchical. The increasing movement of people between churches without regard for denominational affiliation has created a situation where Baptist churches have had to decide whether or not to enrol as members those who have been baptised as infants and who decline to be baptised again. Unable to recognise infant baptism, they either have to insist on the routine rebaptism of these potential new members, or adopt an open policy that allows even unbaptised people to be members; adopting the latter policy, Baptist churches come to be defined as those that are willing to rebaptise, rather than as those that insist upon it. Most, but not all, UK Baptist churches belong to the UK Baptist Union.

Benefice

The post held by an **incumbent**; also the geographic area covered by that post. Historically a benefice consisted of a single **parish**, but a single incumbent may now be responsible for two or more parishes in a so-called 'united' or 'multi-parish' benefice. Combining benefices in this way is the only way to reduce the number of incumbents' posts, and requires the consent of every **patron** and **parochial church council** affected, as well as the diocesan **bishop** (usually taking advice from specially constituted **deanery**, area and diocesan committees) and the Privy Council. The diocesan bishop's alternative is to suspend the benefice, without the consent of any of the above, and appoint a priest-in-charge, who serves without the usual incumbent's privileges (such as security of tenure) and remains directly answerable to the bishop.

Biblical infallibility

The notion that the Bible is literally the word of God, entirely without error in every detail, and therefore the supreme and unquestionable authority in all the topics it covers. Regarded by most **evangelicals** as an essential element of the faith, on the basis that questioning any part of the Bible means giving up on the entire book. Illogically, an exemption is often granted for the first eleven chapters of Genesis, covering (amongst other things) the seven days of creation, Adam and Eve and Noah's flood, and representing about 1 per cent of the whole. The remaining 99 per cent remains entirely infallible, supremely authoritative and fundamentally unquestionable.

Bishop

Traditionally a bishop has sole authority over a **diocese**. The Church of England also has assistant bishops, known as **area** or **suffragan bishops**, who serve under the authority of the diocesan bishop, assisting in the management of the diocese and its staff, and sharing in the tasks reserved exclusively to bishops such as the **ordination** of new clergy. There are currently forty-seven suffragan posts and twenty area posts: all but five of the forty-three diocesan bishops have either suffragan or area assistants. In retirement a former diocesan, suffragan or area bishop can serve as an honorary assistant bishop.

Book of Common Prayer

The title given in the Church of England to the book containing the definitive authorised liturgies of the church. The title was first used in 1549 for the first English-language service book (services were previously in Latin). A second edition followed in 1552, and the current edition dates from 1662. The language is now distinctively archaic. Since 1970 the **General Synod** of the Church of England has had the right to authorise alternative texts for services, for use in parishes that choose them. The **Alternative Service Book 1980** was produced on this basis, replaced in 2000 by a series of volumes known collectively as *Common Worship*. Legally the 1662 Book of Common Prayer remains the definitive text.

Broad church

Classically the centrist party in the Church of England, drawing on influences both catholic and protestant. Evolved into the mid-twentieth century **liberal** centre of the Church of England. Now struggling in the face of rising **evangelical** influence following the collapse of **anglo-catholicism**.

Catholic

In origin, the word catholic means universal or all-embracing. In popular use it is synonymous with Roman Catholic: this use is encouraged by the **Roman Catholic** church itself, which dislikes the label 'Roman Catholic' and prefers to think of itself simply as the catholic church – the one universal and all-embracing **church** – as a claim of primacy amongst the various churches; it then defines the other churches and faiths on its own terms as mistaken by degrees, but forgivable. In principle, however, all **protestant denominations** assert that they are part of the one universal and all-embracing church, differentiating between the visible church of human institutions, and the real or invisible church whose membership list is known to God alone. Most retain a line in their **creed** asserting belief in the one holy catholic church, and in their foundation documents assert their membership of it. For nuance, however, most **protestant denominations** (and **evangelicals** within the Church of England) dislike and avoid the word, because of its association with pre-**reformation** abuses in the Roman Catholic church, but those who feel the reformation went too far (especially in its rejection of the sacraments) warm to the word, and apply it to themselves even when they have very good reasons for remaining separate from the power structures and policies of the Roman Catholic church.

Charismatic

In the contemporary church context this adjective is applied to a particular culture, now absorbed within **evangelicalism,** which places a strong emphasis on the dramatic, including spontaneous dancing and clapping, extempore prayer and preaching, loud and/or emotional music and singing, prophecy, visions and speaking in tongues.

Christening

Technically synonymous with **baptism,** but usually referring to the baptism by sprinkling of a child too young to answer for itself.

Church

By universal consensus the church is the people, not the building. In theology the church is made up of all true believers everywhere, on earth and in heaven. Theologians of the **reformation** era helpfully differentiated between the visible church, of fallible human institutions, and the invisible church, whose membership list is known to God alone. In terms of human institutions, the label is sometimes applied to **denominations** (for example: the **Methodist Church**, the **United Reformed Church**, the Church of England) and sometimes to individual congregations (Saint James's Church, Potter Street Baptist Church). In the **Roman Catholic** church, 'a local church' means a diocese. In the legislation of the Church of England, 'church' means a building.

Church Assembly

Predecessor to the **General Synod**. Formally established by Parliament in 1920 'to deliberate on all matters concerning the Church of England and to make provision in respect thereof'. Its most famous piece of work was one of its earliest: the revised Prayer Book of 1928, rejected by Parliament, provoking the crisis that led eventually to the establishment of the church synodical government system, with General Synod replacing the Church Assembly in 1970.

Congregational

A form of church government whereby authority rests with the local congregation, which can affiliate to a network or **denomination** if it so chooses. The main Congregational denomination in England and Wales merged with the **Presbyterian** denomination to form the **United Reformed Church** in 1972. **Baptist** churches have congregational government, making the Baptist Union the UK's main congregational denomination.

Creed

A formal statement of faith. The earliest Christian creed was 'Jesus is Lord.' **Roman Catholics** and **Anglicans** recognise (and recite) both the Apostles' Creed (the precise origins of which are uncertain) and the Nicene Creed (developed at the Councils of Nicea, AD 325, and Constantinople, AD 381). Both are built on a trinitarian formula (recognition of God the Father, God the Son and God the Holy Spirit). In English the Apostles' Creed runs to just over one hundred words, and the longer Nicene Creed to just over two hundred words.

Curate

Technically any **priest** (or **deacon**) in any **parish** post, including an **incumbent,** but in common use a contraction of 'assistant curate', a junior priest (or deacon) who is answerable not only to the diocesan **bishop** but also to the incumbent of the parish in which he or she is based.

Deacon

The first of three tiers of **ordination** in the Church of England (deacon, **priest** and **bishop**); in practice a probationary year, as the newly ordained are made deacons first, then routinely ordained priest a year later.

Deanery

A group of about fifteen or twenty **parishes** covering a town, part of a city or a network of villages. The clergy of the deanery meet several times a year as the deanery chapter, chaired by one of their own number, the area dean or rural dean.

Denomination

There is no single definition of a denomination, as each denomination defines itself and all other Christian congregations on its own terms; but in common use the word refers to a network of congregations that form a recognisable subdivision within the Christian religion. The Church of England, the **Methodist Church** and the **United Reformed Church** are all recognisable denominations, and similar nationally organised denominations exist in most countries. In the UK the **Baptist** Union is usually assumed to be a denomination, but its member churches are independent, so it is more like a federation than a denomination. Some of the new independent churches belong to highly authoritarian networks but would reject the word denomination. The **Roman Catholic** and Eastern Orthodox churches regard denominationalism as a **protestant** problem and do not identify themselves as denominations.

Diocesan quota

Also called Parish Share. The payment made by a **parish** towards the running costs of the **diocese**. Parishes look after their own buildings, the out-of-pocket working expenses of the clergy, and the local costs of their own activities. The diocese pays clergy salaries, maintains clergy housing, organises the selection and training of the clergy, contributes towards the cost of future clergy pensions, and makes payments to support the national Church of England institutions: all of this is funded largely by quota, which in turn comes largely from the parish collection plate. In law quota remains a voluntary payment, and each diocese is struggling with the question of how to respond as quota collection rates fall.

Diocese

In the Church of England a geographical area about the size of a county with one Church of England cathedral, one diocesan **bishop,** and on average around three hundred **parishes** and two hundred salaried clergy.

Ecclesiology

The theology of what the ideal **church** might be like; and the study (in comparison) of the actual church on earth.

Ecclesiastical

Of or relating to the church.

Ecumenical

Used to describe any movement, organisation or event that brings diverse Christian people together. In the earliest Christian centuries the great international councils of the church were called ecumenical councils. In the post-**reformation** era the word is used whenever two or more **denominations** work together.

Episcopal

Of or relating to a **bishop** or bishops.

Eucharist

The **liturgy** (church service) in which bread and wine are shared in remembrance of Christ. This liturgy is given many different names with different nuances: eucharist is less **catholic** than **mass**, but more catholic than holy communion. All three of these names are avoided by many **protestants**, who prefer communion (without holy), or The Breaking of Bread, or The Lord's Supper.

Evangelical (Evangelicalism, Evangelical Alliance)

Literally, bringer of good news. In Greek the *eu-* prefix means good, and *angel* is to do with messengers and messages, as in angel. *Euangelion* in the Greek New Testament is rendered in English as gospel, or more fashionably as Good News. Luther was content to claim the title Evangelical for his proclamation of the good news that people could find the grace of God without having to obey the corrupt Roman church. Many **Lutheran** churches around the world are officially called Evangelical Lutheran churches, for example the Evangelical Lutheran Church in America, which is the main Lutheran **denomination** in the United States. By nuance, however, the word evangelical now refers to a form of **protestant**ism that is much more extreme than Lutheranism. The Lutheran church in Harlow, Essex, was so embarrassed at having the word Evangelical carved into its main wall as part of its name (the Evangelical Lutheran Church of the Redeemer) that it took render, filled in the eleven letters one by one, sanded off the result and painted it over. In the UK, evangelical culture and its associated beliefs are defined by the Evangelical Alliance and its eleven-point Basis of Faith. Congregations can sign up for membership of the Alliance, whatever their denomination, on assenting to its Basis of Faith. Five hundred and fifty Church of England congregations have signed up, along with almost one thousand **Baptist** congregations and two thousand other congregations from a hundred other denominations and independent networks. Since 2002, the Evangelical Alliance has had its own theological commission, the Alliance Commission on Unity and Truth Among Evangelicals (ACUTE), which prepared the current Basis of Faith, adopted in 2005. The Basis of Faith includes belief in the universal corruption of humankind incurring divine wrath and judgement, the justification of sinners solely through faith in Christ, and the personal and visible return of Jesus Christ to bring eternal life to the redeemed and eternal condemnation to the lost.

Evangelism/Evangelist (Evangelisation)

Literally the bringing of good news/ the bringer of good news. Same derivation as **evangelical** above, but with different contemporary nuances. All churches in principle support evangelism – letting non-churchgoers know about the **church** and its faith – and anyone who participates in that work is technically an evangelist. Confusion between these words and the words evangelical and evangelicalism have led to most churches avoiding using the words, and this in turn has allowed evangelicalism to claim them for its own. Attempting to open up a new front in the nuance wars, the **Roman Catholic** church has adopted the word evangelisation to replace evangelism.

Family Service

Until the 1980s, virtually every **parish** in the Church of England used the services defined by the law of the land: Morning Prayer (Matins), Evening Prayer (Evensong) and Holy Communion. Family Service is not, and never has been, an official service of the Church of England. The title became popular in the early 1980s as a way of promoting services that were attempting to be family-friendly. Often these services would include the minimum requirements to make them legal: technically they would still be services of Morning Prayer or Holy Communion, just rebranded and presented in a more accessible fashion, with modern or child-friendly music, a chattier vicar, and a teaching slot with visual aids in place of a sermon. The brand name is now ubiquitous. In many places it is no more than an indication that Sunday School has been cancelled, but in other places any attempt at retaining the legal minimum content has been abandoned and the entire service is created locally, dependent entirely on the skills and theology of those putting the service together. Family Service culture, in the Church of England, is virtually synonymous with **evangelical** culture.

Flying bishop

Officially known as the Provincial Episcopal Visitors, the Church of England's three flying bishops support those parishes that reject the ministry of women priests.

Fundamentalism

Now used to define any religion that seems to be dangerously out of control, the word was first claimed by one particular group of American **evangelicals** defending five supposedly fundamental principles of evangelical faith against the advance of **liberal** theology. These were: the literal inerrancy of scripture; the divinity of Jesus; the virgin birth; the substitutionary atonement (the death of Jesus in our place to bring about reconciliation with God), and the bodily resurrection of Jesus followed by his bodily ascension into heaven and his imminent return to earth.

General Synod

The parliament of the Church of England since 1970. Arranged in three houses: bishops, clergy and laity. The **house of bishops** is made up of all forty-three diocesan **bishops** and ten **suffragan bishops** (elected by the suffragan bishops from amongst their own number). The house of clergy is made up of 182 clergy elected by the clergy, plus six university chaplains, three service chaplains, one prison chaplain, five cathedral deans, the dean of either Jersey or

Guernsey and two ordained monks or nuns. There are 211 members of the house of laity, elected by members of **deanery synods**, who are in turn elected by **Parochial Church Councils**, plus two lay monks or nuns. The sheer numbers mean that very few deanery synod members have ever met the lay people they elect to General Synod. The full synod of 466 meets residentially for three or four days twice a year, once in London and once in York, or three times a year if the volume of business makes it necessary. Major decisions require the consent of all three houses, sometimes with a two-thirds majority, and often the consent of both the House of Commons and the House of Lords as well.

High church

The **catholic** or **anglo-catholic** influence or party in the Church of England, with elaborate buildings and liturgies and largely catholic theology.

House of Bishops

The forty-three diocesan **bishops** of the Church of England.

Incumbent

The senior **priest** in a **benefice** in the Church of England, having security of tenure and significant authority in the running of the **parish** or parishes of the benefice, as well as legal rights and responsibilities concerning **baptisms**, weddings and funerals in the benefice. Known in most parishes as the **vicar**, and in others as the rector, by historic convention.

Lay person/lay people/laity

Any person who is baptised but not ordained.

Liberal

The name given to a theological movement originating in the universities of northern Germany in the late nineteenth and early twentieth centuries which sought to apply to theology the insights of other disciplines. This included the application of textual analysis to the scriptures, identifying different forms of literature including saga, legend, hagiography, poetry and parable, and further reflection on conventional theological positions using the insights of the sciences including astronomy, biology, psychology and anthropology. Much opposed by the **fundamentalists**, who feared that the faith was being dismantled rather than refreshed with new insights.

Liberal catholic

The dominant influence in the Church of England in the mid-twentieth century, being a combination of **liberal** and **catholic** sensibilities.

Liturgy

The public worship of the **church**; commonly called church services. The word encompasses every aspect of the event, and literally means the work of the people.

Low church

The **protestant** influence or party in the Church of England, with plain buildings and **liturgies** and largely protestant theology.

Lutheran

Literally of or relating to Martin Luther, an important leader in the early stages of the **reformation**; in formal contemporary use, the name given to any **church** or **denomination** adhering to the Augsburg Confession of 1530, one of the earliest clear statements of the purposes and intentions of churches breaking away from Roman authority. The clarity and formality of the Augsburg Confession (twenty-eight articles running to fourteen thousand words) make global Lutheranism one of the most cohesive global denominational networks, united by a statement of faith rather than a global authority structure.

Mass

The main **Roman Catholic** and **anglo-catholic** name for the **liturgy** in which bread and wine are shared in remembrance of Christ. This basic liturgy is known elsewhere – in order of nuance from **catholic** to **protestant** – as the Eucharist, Holy Communion, Communion, The Lord's Supper and The Breaking of Bread. Much theological ill-will derives from the arguments over what actually happens to the bread and the wine at the mass, on account of the recorded words of Jesus when he broke bread and gave it to his disciples at supper the night before his crucifixion: 'This is my body, which is given for you; do this in remembrance of me.'

Methodist Church

Methodism emerged in the eighteenth century under the leadership of John and Charles Wesley, both of whom were Church of England clergy. They used preaching, singing and a call to personal holiness as key elements in an evangelical revival. On the fringes of legality, they established independent preaching houses, and died still hoping their movement might continue within the Church of England. After their deaths, the Yearly Conference of the People Called Methodists quickly declared its preaching houses to be chapels and its key preachers to be ministers, and began organising its own services of holy communion, thereby ceasing to be part of the Church of England and becoming a new **denomination**. Methodism subsequently split into several factions, reuniting in the early twentieth century.

Authority lies with the annual national Methodist Conference.

New Wine Network

A leading UK **charismatic-evangelical** network, currently drawing twenty-five thousand people to its residential summer conferences each year, mostly from within the Church of England. At the charismatic end of the charismatic–evangelical spectrum.

Ordination

The process of setting people apart for service within the church, establishing good order by assigning people to different orders of ministry (order and ordination share a common root). **Bishops** do the ordaining, by laying their hands on the heads of each ordinand in turn at an ordination service. In the Church of England there are three orders of ministry: an individual can be ordained up to three times, as **deacon** first, then as **priest**, then as bishop. The newly ordained usually serve one year as a deacon before being ordained priest. Amongst other things deacons are not permitted to lead services of holy communion; in practice the year spent as a deacon serves as a probationary year. The public debate about the ordination of women in the Church of England the 1980s and 1990s was about the ordination of women to the priesthood: women had been serving as deaconesses since 1861 (an order now closed to new entrants), and as deacons since 1987 (creating a temporary revival of interest in the role and purpose of a deacon); the first ordinations of women to the priesthood in the Church of England took place in 1994. The Church of England's order of bishops remains closed to women. This threefold order of ministry is an **anglican** peculiarity: **protestant** churches have a single order of ministry (known simply as ministers) or reject the idea of ordination altogether; the **Roman Catholic** church classically had dozens of minor and intermediate orders and abolished most of them at the Second Vatican Council, leaving just bishops and priests; it is now experimenting with the ordination of unsalaried married men as deacons. Deacons are ordained by the bishop alone, priests are ordained by the bishop and other existing priests together, all crowding around and laying hands on the new priest's head, and bishops are ordained by existing bishops together, usually three, sometimes a crowd.

Parish

A geographical area for which an **incumbent** is responsible.

Parochial Church Council

The council of **lay people** in a **parish**, elected by an annual meeting of those on the church electoral roll, for specific purposes relating to the operation of the Church of England in the parish. Not to be confused with a parish council, which is the lowest tier of state local government. The two types of parish do not necessarily share boundaries, and are sometimes called civil and **ecclesiastical** for clarity.

Patron

The person, office or body that appoints an **incumbent** (a vicar or a rector) when the post falls vacant. Every **benefice** has its own patron or patronage arrangement; for example, where several benefices have been combined there is often a large patronage committee, or an arrangement whereby different patrons have one turn each in rotation. Patronages are property in English law: they are transferred by deed or by inheritance. Patronages are often used to exert long-term partisan influence on a **parish**. Many have been transferred over the years to explicitly partisan patronage boards, established for the purpose. Parishes now have a veto on the patron's nomination, and the patron's rights lapse six months into a vacancy.

Presbyterian

A form of church government based on various tiers of authority, each having its own set of rights and responsibilities, including the local congregation, the meeting of local ministers (known as the presbytery), area synods and national assemblies. The precise sets of rights and responsibilities given to each tier of authority make each presbyterian **denomination** unique, and Scottish presbyterianism has split several times as a result. In the UK the

United Reformed Church is the main denomination organised along presbyterian lines, although its structures are highly centralised compared to many presbyterian denominations. The United Reformed Church was formed in 1972 by the merger of the main **congregational** and Presbyterian denominations in England and Wales.

Priest

Virtually every ordained minister in the Church of England has been ordained priest. The word is used by **Roman Catholics** of their ordained ministers, but not by **protestants** of theirs, so its use in the Church of England, whilst technically universal, is in practice partisan: protestants (and the broad centre) avoid it from ordination day onwards, using the words **vicar, curate** and minister instead, while **anglo-catholics** use it as their title of first choice (parish priest, assistant priest) to describe their clergy.

Protestant

Generally the name given to all churches that are neither **Roman Catholic** nor Eastern Orthodox, being the churches that emerged from the **reformation** having shed their loyalty to Rome, and other churches established since. The name derives from a protest made in April 1529 by representatives of the reforming region around Wittenberg to the Emperor of Germany against his renewed attempts to suppress Lutheran reforms.

Quota

See **diocesan quota**.

Rector

A title used for the **incumbent** in some Church of England **parishes**, in place of (and equivalent to) the more common title of **vicar**. Each parish uses one or the other consistently, by historic convention. An incumbent by either name has security of tenure and significant authority in the running of the parish. In so-called team parishes, fashionable for a while in the 1970s, the senior **priest** is called the team rector and most of the junior priests, previously known as **curates** or assistant curates, are called team vicars. The team vicars are said to have incumbent status (status being very important in the Church of England) but in reality only the team rector is an incumbent, and in some team parishes even the team rector does not have security of tenure.

Reform

A **protestant fundamentalist** movement within the Church of England, opposed to the **ordination** of women and active in the campaign against the acceptance of homosexuality. Reform is happy to condemn individual Church of England **bishops** by name, declaring them unfit to supervise clergy who are members of Reform unless they (the bishops) assent to Reform doctrines and demands. One to watch in the impending break-up of the Church of England; equally, might disappear without trace: better at making headlines than winning seats on synod.

Reformation

The sixteenth-century movement that saw the western church split into factions loyal to Rome and factions separated from Rome.

Resolutions A, B and C

Resolutions A and B were included in the legislation for the **ordination** of women as **priests** in the Church of England in 1993. Resolution C was conceived later that year by an Act of Synod allowing further concessions to parishes which had passed either Resolution A or Resolution B. Resolution A: *This Parochial Church Council would not accept a woman as the minister who presides at or celebrates the Holy Communion or pronounces the absolution in the Parish.* Resolution B: *This parochial church council would not accept a woman as the incumbent or priest-in-charge of the benefice or as a team vicar for the benefice.* The Episcopal Ministry Act of Synod 1993 granted **Parochial Church Councils** the right to petition the diocesan **bishop** to the effect that **episcopal** duties in the **parish** should be carried out by the Provincial Episcopal Visitor. The Provincial Episcopal Visitors became known unofficially as the **flying bishops,** and the petitioning became known unofficially (but universally) as Resolution C.

Roman Catholic

It is anachronistic to use this phrase to refer to the church in the west before the **reformation**. Five hundred years before the Reformation, the church had split into east and west, with the western church loyal to Rome; but for people in western Europe there was only one church and it was simply the church. It was only after the reformation that it became necessary to define church loyalties in terms other than western or eastern. Henry VIII condemned 'Romanists', not catholics, and considered himself a catholic to his deathbed. The phrase Roman Catholic is now used to describe those churches that are directly linked, structurally, to the Vatican: both loyal to and recognised by Rome. It is not a term much liked by the Roman Catholic church itself, which prefers to think of itself simply as the catholic church.

Sacrament

For **protestants,** an outward and visible sign of an inward and spiritual grace. For **catholics,** the real presence of God in the world in tangible, material form. Generally limited in protestantism to **baptism** and holy communion; much wider in catholicism. The number of catholic sacraments has gone up and down over the centuries, but has settled at seven: the mass, baptism, confirmation (by a **bishop** on the personal declaration of faith by an individual previously baptised as an infant), holy orders (**ordination**), absolution (the declaration of forgiveness by a priest), anointing with oil for healing, and marriage.

Suffragan bishop

A junior **bishop,** serving as an assistant to a diocesan bishop.

United Reformed Church

The main **Congregational denomination** in England and Wales merged with the **Presbyterian** denomination to form the United Reformed Church in 1972.

Vicar

The title given to the **incumbent** in most Church of England **parishes,** being the senior **priest** in the parish with security of tenure and significant authority in the running of the parish. In some parishes, by historic convention, the incumbent has the title **rector** instead of vicar. In so-called team parishes, fashionable for a while in the 1970s, the senior priest is called the team rector and most of the junior priests, previously known as **curates** or assistant curates, are called team vicars. The team vicars are said to have incumbent status (status being very important in the Church of England) but in reality only the team rector is an incumbent, and in some team parishes even the team rector does not have security of tenure.